GARDEN OF EDEN?

Pete Rolving pushed open the control room door of the *Daedalus*. "You better come," he said. "I got an answer to the radio signal."

That was good news. I shot to my feet and I could see the relief in Nathan's face. But Pete was quick to jump in on top of our elation.

"They don't make much sense," he said. "In fact, they don't make any sense at all."

He was already moving back along the corridor. "They're like children. Half the time I can't tell what they say. They made contact in response to the alarm, but I don't think they know what they're doing at all. I get the impression that they think it's God talking. They keep saying 'Thank God' over and over.

"Something," said Pete Rolving, as we reached the radio, "is wrong."

And that understatement was the beginning of a recontact ecological puzzle that almost couldn't be solved.

Critical Threshold

BRIAN M. STABLEFORD

DAW BOOKS, INC.

DONALD A. WOLLHEIM, PUBLISHER

1301 Avenue of the Americas
New York, N. Y.   10019

FIRST PRINTING, FEBRUARY 1977

1 2 3 4 5 6 7 8 9

PRINTED IN U.S.A.

Chapter 1

I collected the cards and began to shuffle them half-heartedly, wondering whether I could squeeze a few last drops of competitive enthusiasm from my turgid brain. It didn't seem likely.

Karen watched me. She was fully awake and comfortable. I was *too* fully awake, and not so comfortable.

"You want to play again?" I asked.

She didn't. She shook her head. "You could use some sleep," she said. "I have to be here. I'm on eight hour shifts for the duration. I don't need anyone to keep me company. Do you know what time it is?"

My eyes went to the clock and stared blindly at its face.

"No," I told her. "To be quite honest, I don't. I see where the hands are pointing, but I just don't see that it means anything. How can it? It didn't even make sense last time we made landfall—it didn't match local time, it wasn't even registering the right length of day. It's been ticking away merrily even since we left Earth, but it doesn't even tell us what time it is on Earth. It isn't any time at all on Earth. We're taking a short cut through spacetime, dodging round the laws of physics while their backs are turned. We're outside the whole fabric of existence. So what the hell does the clock think it's telling us?"

She sighed. "It *ought* to be telling you that it's time to get some sleep," she said.

"Well it isn't getting the message across."

5

"Having trouble with our circadian rhythms?" she said, blandly.

I shrugged. "Circadian rhythms weren't evolved to cope with faster-than-light travel. Mine don't like it. They rebel against the shallow lies told by the clock."

"Claustrophobia," she said. "You should have been screened for that before we took off."

"It's not the physical confinement I object to," I told her. "It's the intellectual confinement. My mind's in a cage and it doesn't like it. I just don't know how the others manage to regulate themselves so easily. I don't work that way."

According to the clock it was nearly two o'clock in the morning. We'd been in flight for about two weeks, out of Floria heading for Dendra. It wasn't just that I'd become used to Florian time, with days that weren't twenty-four hours long, that made an absolute fool of the stubborn atomic clock aboard the *Daedalus*. It was something more—something about the experience of interstellar flight itself.

Karen didn't understand. She wasn't about to make any attempt to understand, but was simply content to be amused. She was crew, and her life was ruled by standard time even when we made landfall. She had the timetable written into her nervous system.

"What do you think about?" I asked. "When you're out here on watch, obliged to be awake when everyone else is asleep? It's not as if you had anything to do except check the tell-tales every now and again. You don't even have to be in the cockpit. How do you occupy your thoughts?"

"*That*'s what's wrong with you," she said, ignoring the question. "Utter boredom. Hell, Alex—it's only three weeks at a time. We were on Floria for a year, we'll likely be on Dendra for another. You ought to be glad of three weeks rest in between."

"It's not the length of time," I said. "It's the emptiness of it. Trying to fill it is such an effort. We do our work, and then we make a little extra, or do it again. We play word games, card games, sex games. And somehow it just doesn't fill up. There's a perpetual sense of dislocation."

"Oh, there's that," she agreed. "Unnatural. Cutting

corners. Arriving before we set off, relatively speaking, and still spending three weeks doing it. But don't let your imagination overact. You can't face the thing with common sense, because the universe doesn't work according to common sense notions. It's just something you have to get used to. If it really bothers you, take something."

I shook my head.

"It's funny," she said, "This doesn't bother me at all—being in the ship, in ultraspace. You know when I start getting dislocated? The day we stop. When we land on some crazy world that feels almost like Earth, with air almost like Earth's, which looks almost like Earth, you know —so similar, but so different. *That* throws me. When the days and the nights stop agreeing with the clock, with *real* time."

I grinned, leaning back in my chair to stretch my arms. "One of us," I murmured, "is backwards."

"Well," she said, "I can honestly look myself in the eye and say 'it isn't me'."

I smiled politely at the wordplay. Word games. Trivial, but they helped.

"You didn't answer my question," I said. "What do you think about, when the schedule leaves you on your own?"

"Anything," she said. "Everything. I don't get hypnotized waiting for the tell-tales to wink. I read, I talk to insomniacs. Maybe Pete holds mystic communion with the machines and the infinite, but I'm boring. I just do what's there to be done, take it easy, make it easy."

Maybe I can make it easy too, I thought. Maybe there is some easy way to stop the idea that we were alone and insignificant in an unimaginable gulf preying on my consciousness. Not to mention my subconscious.

Sometimes, in the thin spaces of the *Daedalus*, I wondered whether I was really cut out for deep space and the recontact mission. It was something I'd been waiting all my life to do, but that's not necessarily a guarantee of competence. I was supposed to be an expert on alien environments, but the environment of the ship itself— perhaps the mission itself—sometimes seemed a little *too* alien. More alien, anyhow, then the colony worlds themselves.

It was me, I decided, that was backwards. Karen made more sense.

"If you're going to sit up and challenge your mind with great philosophical questions of our time," she said, "then you can make the coffee while you're doing it. I'll be back in two minutes."

She disappeared in the direction of the control panel.

I made the coffee, and put the cards away. When she came back I was staring at a spot on the ceiling.

"Isn't it amazing," I commented, "that even in the most rigorously sterile environments, spots appear on the ceiling."

"And you also get dirt under your fingernails," she said. "Let's for God's sake not bore each other to death. Talk about something sensible. Help me overcome my inevitable dislocation, tell me Dendra's guilty secrets."

I looked at her pensively, slightly reluctant to be jerked out of my desolate mood. She stared at me. She had quite a powerful stare. I was tempted to fix my gaze on the ceiling again.

"You've read the reports," I said. "You know exactly as much as I do."

"No chance," she replied. "I read the reports, they're words. But to you, they mean something. They build up a picture in your mind, an idea of what it's like. I just get a blur. I'm a mechanic, not an ecological romantic."

"We all have our problems," I commented, dryly. But I wasn't unwilling to talk about Dendra. I *did* have a picture, of sorts. Trying to describe the picture would probably help to clarify it. Sometimes you don't know what you think until you try to explain it.

"It's a forest," I said. "A very, very big forest. Not homogeneous, geographically speaking, but continuous. One vast expanse of trees running right around the planet. The planet's unusual because it's too ordinary—you know what I mean?"

She nodded. "No axial tilt. Spins in the plane of its orbit. Two moons, both tiny, in the same plane. Very orderly. No seasonal changes to speak of."

"More than that," I said. "There's one vast continent girdling the world around the equator, stretching north and south to the forty-third parallel, or thereabouts, on either side. There are two large polar seas with jagged edges. Such wonderful symmetry. Low altitude airstreams blow more or less constantly from the poles towards the equator—gigantic convection currents which bring rain to feed the forest and the rivers. All of which means that conditions are very stable all over the land surface. Remarkably so. The temperate zones are very temperate, and the climate changes according to a smooth progression as you go north or south toward the tropics. Comfortable, reliable."

"Like Floria."

"Not like Floria. Floria's supposed stability is really just lethargy. No tides, no definite motor of change—but change is going on, and there's a wide range of conditions geographically speaking. There are forests and deserts and marshes and savannah. But on Dendra, there's only the forest. It stretches everywhere, and only the tallest mountains have slopes above the tree line where virtually nothing can flourish. Dendra is just one vast, continuous habitat.

"And it's teeming with life. Thousands of species. Insects, vertebrates, a fuller range than Earth. Life's been hard on Earth, and a lot of potential groups never made it. But on Dendra, the evolution of the forest has stabilized the whole pattern of change within it. The larger, fiercer creatures that seem to dominate much of Earth's evolutionary history aren't there. In a forest, it pays to be small. But the sequence of physical development is strikingly similar. You can't use terms like *insect* and *mammal* exactly when you talk about an alien life-system—you're always drawing analogies rather than making a rational classification—but on Dendra there are insects which are for all the world like Earth insects, and mammals like Earth mammals. There are birds, there are frogs, and some things we'll have to make up new names for. But by and large, the animal population of Dendra is strikingly similar to the animal population of any subtropical forest on Earth—only more so. And the whole planet is one enormously complex community, in ecological terms."

I paused, waiting for her to stop me because I was being boring, or to ask questions, or simply to invite me to go on.

I think she was amused by the way the words flowed:
a little too fast, a little less than certain.

"So?" she prompted.

"The implications," I said, "are legion. You've seen
what the survey team wrote in terms of general conclusions. They advised against colonization."

"I know what they advised," she said. "But I don't
know why. It seemed, by all accounts, a very hospitable
world. And they were overruled—a colony was sent out."

"It's difficult," I said. "Maybe the survey scientists themselves couldn't put forward an itemized list of reasons
why Dendra was unsuitable. It's just that the whole thing
has the wrong *feel*.

"One point is that there seems to be a relationship between the stability of communities and their complexity.
And there's a sort of feedback loop which means that
the more complex a situation becomes the more stable it
can become, and if it does become more stable it finds
extra opportunities for complexification. On Earth, the
loop isn't important because changes in circumstances—
weather, geological factors, etc.—put a limit on stability.
But on Dendra that limit is very different. The opportunities for stabilization and complexification are much
greater. Unless, of course, an invader moves in from outside—a human invader."

"You mean they might trigger changes which would
upset the whole system?"

"Maybe . . . or maybe the whole system would be so
efficient that it wouldn't permit them to make changes
at all. Or maybe nothing. It's the sort of factor which just
can't be weighed. You can't find out until you try. And if
you find out that the answer is disaster. . . ."

"It's already too late."

"Quite so."

"You think the colony may have failed?"

"I'm not about to lay any bets either way."

"You must have an opinion."

I shook my head firmly. "On the contrary. I *mustn't*
form an opinion. That's the trap. When you don't have
enough data, you have to be content to be undecided.
That's why the survey report ran into trouble with the
UN. The men who compiled the report were undecided,
because they didn't have enough information to decide—

but the UN wouldn't accept that. The survey simply reported a vast profusion of unknown factors—not simply because of the question of the stability of the Dendran ecosphere, but its complexity too. The survey team had a limited time. There was no way they could *begin* a full investigation of a life-system as complex as Dendra's. They looked hard, and everything they saw looked good, but it was what they never got a chance to look at that worried them most. They could no more compile a full dossier on Dendra's life-system than they could count and classify every star in the known universe. That's a job for a lifetime—a hundred lifetimes. And it would never be wholly done. What the survey team had to do was guess the whole pattern from the pieces they had. Usually, teams feel confident enough to say that they have an educated guess, a good guess. The Dendran team didn't feel that confident. They had an educated guess, all right, but they didn't feel that it was a good one."

"If that's the case," she said, "why *did* they send a colony to Dendra?"

"Political minds work to a different set of criteria," I said, with vague traces of sarcasm. "And in addition, there was probably a little double-dealing. Ask Nathan. He could read between those particular lines far better than I can."

"Nathan's sleeping the sleep of the just," she pointed out.

Just what? I wondered. But I didn't say it.

"If you like," I said, "I'll tell you what my nasty little mind suspects. But I could be wrong. Political waters run deep. And murky. I may be doing someone an injustice."

And, I added, under my breath, pigs might have had wings in those days.

"I'm listening," she said. "It all helps to fill up the time."

"Look at it this way," I said. "Exploratory vessels go out looking for Earth-type worlds. When one of them finds one it makes a few elementary observations from orbit, and then goes on somewhere else. It isn't equipped to land. When it gets home, all its data are examined. The worlds which might prove hospitable are sorted out, and survey teams go out—at colossal expense —to land, stay about a year, and make a supposedly-thorough examination of the prospects for human habitation. They can't find out everything, but they use their time as efficiently as possible, and the idea is that they should find out *enough*. Only what's 'enough'. Who can tell? And—more important, perhaps—who gets to decide?

"It costs a hell of a lot to do a survey. It doesn't even end when the team returns—there are more experiments to be done with material brought back. This is long and tedious because it has to be done under strict quarantine —a precaution which, though necessary, does limit the scope of the investigation.

"At the end of it all it's a grade A tragedy if the scientists come back and say: 'Sorry, it's no good.' The trouble is, though, that they can never really say: 'Great, it's perfect.' The best they can do is come up with an estimate of the possible risk—a guess which, though it be the most educated guess in the world, remains a guess. Things like the organic correspondence factor between Earth and the alien world can be measured exactly, but that isn't necessarily anything to do with the probability that a colony will survive. But someone, or a whole series of someones, has to take the hard data, weigh it up, and come up with a figure.

"That's science, even if it is a bit rough-hewn and speculative. But now we move out of the realms of science. Because another someone, or a whole series of other someones, has to make the decision as to what level of probability constitutes an *acceptable* risk. Is an eighty per cent chance of success worth taking? Or an eighty-five per cent chance? How about eighty-one, or maybe eighty-one and a half? This kind of political bargaining is made all the more difficult because the probabilities themselves can't pretend to be accurate, and certainly not precise to one or two per cent.

"The politicians take into account all kinds of extraneous factors like the cost of mounting a colony project, the cash they've already ploughed in, the climate of public opinion and the pressures of all kinds of power-groups as they're felt at that particular moment. All these things may influence the critical threshold—the level of acceptable risk.

"Now, the reports offered by the Dendra team were

more uncertain than almost any other set. In this particular case the team didn't feel they had enough data. But can you imagine what a bureaucrat would say to a scientist who said: 'Well, we've gone through the whole procedure, and we just can't come up with a figure.' That's not what bureaucrats pay scientists for. The survey team had to provide an answer, so they turned one in, along with the qualification that in this particular case the estimate was less confident than usual. The figure they turned in was below the critical threshold, and so, in effect, was advice against attempting colonization.

"But it seems—and I only say *seems*—that the political mind didn't quite approach the issue in the way the scientists anticipated. Imagine a committee of bureaucrats looking at the report. They think: 'We've put an awful lot of money into this for a negative result; and we haven't sent a colony ship out for some time. We're under pressure. And look at this here: it says that this estimate is only tentative. As it is, it's not *far* below the critical threshold, and if the scientists aren't sure, well then the *real* figure might be *above* the critical threshold. Can we afford to abandon this world because the scientists are hesitant? Wouldn't it be ridiculous if we rejected an ideal world because the survey team doesn't think they had long enough to look around? Is there a single scrap of hard evidence that this world may prove inhospitable?'

"And the answer, of course, is no. So what happens?"

"They send a colony anyway," said Karen.

"Wrong," I said. "The political mind moves in mysterious ways its wonders to perform. What they do is to *pass the buck*. They refuse to come to a firm decision. They don't back up the risk-estimate provided by the scientists, and they do their best to discredit it. But they also won't take on to themselves the responsibility of mounting a colony project.

"And so the thing passes out of normal channels, and becomes a special case. Special cases are the bread and butter of professional politicians, because they can be shaped to fit specific and momentary needs—party needs, personal needs—it all depends who catches the buck and gets to slice it. I think Dendra was used in some back-handed political maneuver. What actually happened was that a cut-price colony was planned. Fewer ships than usual, less cash spent on supplies and equipment. The responsibility for the cut-price aspect certainly wasn't accepted by the usual UN planning authority, and probably not by the guy who actually arranged it. It was probably shifted on to the colonists themselvss. Some particular group which had been agitating for a different system of emigration-selection, or even an organization of would-be emigrants who wanted to go *as* a group, were bought off with the offer of a sub-standard world. 'Here, you can have this one. It's rated below threshold, but don't worry about that—just these conservative scientists. It's really okay, but naturally you go at your own risk. Officially, we can't let you go; but officially, of course, you'd have to go through the normal balloting procedure, which is exactly what you want to avoid. Best of luck; and goodbye forever.'

"You see the theme?"

"You have a nasty mind, Alex," she said.

"Haven't *you?*" I countered.

"Oh sure," she replied. "I believe every word. It's not quite what shows up in the reports, though. There's no evidence."

"Look at the colony list," I said. "The cut-price aspect is obvious in the way the ships were crowded and under-supplied. The get-rid-of-the-agitators-at-their-own-risk aspect isn't so clear, but look at the names of the colonists. One hundred per cent Euroamerican. If they were selected by standard ballot the laws of probability were on holiday that week. You want to bet those ships weren't filled by invitation to certain people with significantly louder voices than their less troublesome brethren from nations whose influence in UN affairs wasn't so great in that wonderful Golden Age?"

"You could be right," she agreed.

"See what Nathan thinks," I said. "If he reads between the lines the way I do . . ."

"The last thing he'd do would be to start broadcasting his findings. He'd keep quiet about it."

I thought about that, and decided that it might well be so. Nathan, after all, was their kind of animal. A political mind, moving in its own secret orbit around the truth.

"You think they shouldn't have colonized Dendra?" she asked.

Again, I retreated to my non-committal pedestal. "We'll find out who was wrong and who was lucky when we get there," I said. "Not before."

"And if it's failed?"

"We find out *why* it failed. That's vital. We have to know where the thinking went wrong, and how. We have to know just why the educated guess wasn't educated enough."

"I could almost believe," she said, "that you want this colony to have failed. And for the right reason—some little thing that the survey team didn't find because they didn't have the time. You want to vindicate the scientists who put in the low probability estimate."

"That's garbage," I said, dourly. "If that colony has failed, it will be a tragedy on a big scale."

"Not your tragedy, Alex."

"Everybody's tragedy," I insisted.

"I still think you have mixed feelings," she persisted.

"My feelings are always mixed," I said. "Just like everybody else's. But not that kind of mixture."

Her eyes were fixed on my face, as if she were trying to see right into my skull, like Mariel. But Karen hadn't any advantages of that kind. She had to take my word for what I was thinking.

"And yet," she said, "it's you that can't sleep at night."

I grunted, dismissing the point as irrelevant, though I wasn't wholly sure that it was. Karen, of course, had long since abandoned any concern over man's inhumanity to man (or woman). She took it all in her stride. She had a hard heart. She saved her sympathies for personal matters, and could withdraw it if and when the need arose. Sometimes, I wished I had her detachment.

Only sometimes.

"We could have *real* problems on Dendra," she said, idly. "Not so childishly easy as on Floria."

I smiled at that, largely because it was intended to make me smile. But I was still taking it seriously.

Her eyes strayed briefly to the clock. It was the barest of glances, confirming what she already knew.

"Time to check that we haven't blown up," she said, getting to her feet. She paused slightly as she turned away.

I stayed put for a second, then shrugged. "Maybe I can

muster enough lethargy to get me to sleep," I said, getting up. And I added to lighten the note of our parting: "Suppose we are blowing up?"

"Don't worry about *that*," she said, ironically. "We're outside spacetime. The universe won't even notice we've gone."

It was a comforting thought.

Chapter 2

I hadn't intended that what I said to Karen about Dendra should be in strict confidence. I knew the rumor would get around, even if I didn't help it. I also suspected that Nathan Parrick might not approve. I wasn't really surprised when he sought me out for a confidential word.

It was some days later, shortly before we were scheduled to reach our destination. I was in my room, scanning the reports for the nth time. I was just feeding data into my head and letting my imagination go to work, trying to anticipate problems. Sometimes I can be a real glutton for punishment.

I was reading the atmosphere analysis, and marveling at its complexity. It wasn't the gas mixture that was important—that had to be fairly standard in order to qualify the world for a second look—but the abundance of organic traces. There was a fourteen page list of complex molecules drifting around in minute quantities, detected by mechanical olfactory apparatus. About three dozen were deadly poisons, some were ataractic, several hallucinogenic, three were powerfully narcotic and nearly a hundred unknown. They were all biological products and all biodegradable. They couldn't accumulate in living tissue and weren't present in anywhere near active concentrations. They were just sufficient to scent the air. Oddly enough, the olfactory analysis, though magnificent in scope, missed out on one little detail.

It didn't say whether the overall smell was pleasant or not.

That's the trouble with mechanical devices. They miss out on the important things.

I was looking through the individual molecule-counts, trying to find a freak high enough to worry about. Sometimes the incidence of such trace factors is very variable, and they can build up very quickly to toxic levels, especially in the pollen season. Of such things are disasters made.

I wasn't finding anything, because Dendra didn't *have* a pollen season. There wasn't any kind of cycle at all. All natural processes were continuous.

When Nathan interrupted me I was pleased to see him. It can be frustrating, looking for something that isn't there.

"We're in normal space again," he said, pleasantly. "We'll be in orbit very soon."

"Welcome back to spacetime," I said, dryly.

I got along well enough with Nathan. It had become obvious on Floria that we operated from different conceptual standpoint, but there had been no real clash of opinions since the troubled period when we had landed on Floria and precipitated an abortive rebellion. Once things had settled down and our goals coincided perfectly, we could happily work away in our respective spheres without conflict. We both suspected, however, that the potential for more conflict was still implicit in our attitudes.

"I hear," he said, coming straight to the point, "that you have your doubts about what we might find on Dendra."

"Haven't we all?" I replied, stalling. "We'll be there soon. Then we can all find out."

"I wanted to talk to you first," he said.

I sighed, and moved along the bunk. "Sit down," I invited.

He sat.

"Do you think we need a referee?" I asked.

He refused to be amused. "We land tomorrow," he said.

"All being well. I think it might be wiser if we didn't take down too many preconceived notions about what we might find there."

I saw the point of the eleventh hour approach. He wanted to undermine the ideas that my nasty mind had come up with—or the attitude born of them—at the right strategic moment.

"It's okay," I assured him. "I'm not going down there with a bee in my bonnet about uncovering evidence to crucify a bunch of long-dead political cowboys. I have my priorities in order."

"I know that. What I want to try to avoid, before it crops up, is the kind of communication-breakdown we suffered on Floria. I'd like to agree, if we can, on the principles we work on."

I folded up the reports and stacked them neatly on my knee.

"State your principles," I invited, "and I'll tell you which ones I agree with."

"You're not being very helpful."

"True," I admitted.

"It seems to me," he said, "that you're anticipating a conflict of opinions before there's any need for it. You seem to be assuming that my approach to this world— *whatever* the situation we find there—is going to be radically different from yours."

I shook my head. "If you think that's because of the things I've deduced about the way the Dendra colony was set up, you're wrong. It's not just Dendra, it's everywhere. Our approaches *are* different. You're here to write propaganda. I'm here to help. Well, okay, it's not for me to reason why. I'm not going to interfere with your work, and you won't interfere with mine. But you can't expect me to declare solemnly that I'll agree with what you have to say and do. If we find Dendra— or any other colony—in grave difficulties, then I'm not going to misrepresent the fact in my reports."

"I'm not talking about misrepresentation," he said. "And you're jumping way ahead of me. This assumption of implicit hostility is a handicap to the whole mission, and *that's* what I want to talk about. We're on the same side. We ought to be able to work together."

I had to admit, even to myself, that the prejudice I felt

against Nathan was really an emotional one. I didn't even dislike him personally—I just disliked the kind of man I thought he was. I ought to have been able to put the prejudice aside, but it wasn't easy. It didn't make it any easier, either, that he could come to me and ask me to put it aside.

"I came out here," I said, "to do a job. To recontact the colonies and give them whatever help I could. I believe that we should reinstitute a space program, if not to colonize new worlds, at least to give proper support to the ones already colonized. But you're here to make what we do into a big story—something to be used for propaganda purposes, to make a new space program acceptable to the world. So we want the same thing, but not the same way. I don't want a new space program simply because someone managed to sell the idea in the political marketplace, with the corollary assumption that someone at some future date might sell the idea of abandoning it again. I don't think the matter belongs to the political marketplace at all. I think we should begin the space program again for reasons which go much deeper than that—because we need to become an interstellar community. The reason you and I don't work on the same wavelength is that I'm committed and you're just a professional doing a job, without even believing in it. Your idea of need isn't the same as mine."

He let me run on and finish, and he even left a decent interval to make sure I was completely through.

Then he said: "I was hired as a professional, to do a professional job. So were you. You aren't here because you're a committed man but because you're good at your job. Pete Rolving and Karen Karelia are here because they can fly a starship as well as anyone else. Conrad Silvian and Linda Beck are here because, like you, they're totally capable in handling their equipment and analyzing ecological problems. Nobody was hired for their ideals, Alex. It's ridiculous to think that they should have been."

"Maybe so," I said. I didn't add anything else, just let it hang stubbornly.

"You may not think the political marketplace operates the right way," he went on, "but it operates. It's the place where things are decided, and in practical terms there is no other. It's the only place where ideas—and principles, and needs, and moralities—*can* be bought and sold."

"I know."

"But you insist on making it difficult for yourself."

"It *is* difficult," I said. "That's the way it is all right. But I can't accept it and capitulate with it just because it exists. I can't square it with my conscience. You can. You find it all too easy to adopt the stance that's handed out to you by the *status quo*. Okay. That's you. But it isn't me and it never will be."

The atmosphere in the cabin seemed thick. Most of the tension was on my side. He was still relaxed. He didn't hold it against me. Much.

"I was screened by the UN," I pointed out. "They selected me, warts and all."

"Don't you think that you owe them something, then?" he said, with a casual cutting edge. "A duty to do your job without the emotional extras."

"Is that what we're arguing about?" I asked. "Emotional extras?"

"If you like," he replied.

It was no use reminding him that on Floria things had worked out fine. I hadn't paid much attention to the instructions laid down for us, but it had worked out—in the end. But he wouldn't concede that point. From his point of view, I'd done it all wrong, had *been* in the wrong. It's like backing a winning horse against the form. No serious student of probability will ever admit you did the right thing even while he watches you count your money.

"Look, Alex," he said. "There's no point working up a sweat. I came here to try and prevent this kind of thing happening on the ground. We may have differences, but let's keep them in second place. The mission comes first."

"What do you want from me?" I said. "What do I have to promise?"

"All I ask," he said, "is that when we land you take whatever situation we find as it comes. No judgments. No condemnations. Never mind who gets the credit or who gets the blame. Just do what we came to do, okay?"

"In a calm, detached, professional manner?"

"In a calm, detached, professional manner," he echoed. He was dead serious.

"The way I work," I said, "is to get involved. I don't solve problems by clinical analysis and aloof meditation. I have to be in amongst them. Feeling them."

He didn't sigh. He didn't show any trace of annoyance. Maybe he'd expected it. In any case, it seemed that he knew when to leave things be.

He pointed to the files.

"Find anything?" he asked, levelly. He could have said something along the lines of 'What do your feelings tell you,' and made it sarcastic. He didn't. He was keeping it neutral. He really did want a peace pact.

I thought maybe it was time to climb down just a little. No harm in making things a little easier, on the surface.

"I don't know," I said. "I'm just absorbing it all. I won't be able to read anything into it until I see it on the ground. Twenty minutes in the forest will probably tell me as much as three weeks combing the reports."

"Why comb them then?"

I allowed myself a tiny smile. "It's *because* I've combed them so thoroughly that twenty minutes on the ground will be able to tell me so much more. The way you get to see so much is standing on the shoulders of giants, remember?"

He was ready to smile, too.

He stood up, but before he could reach out to open the door someone else did it for him. It was Pete Rolving, apparently in too much of a hurry to bother knocking.

"You better come," he said. "I got an answer to the radio signal."

That was good news. I shot to my feet, and I could see the relief in Nathan's face. Obiously he'd been worried about the prospect of getting no answer at all.

But Pete was quick to jump in on top of our elation. "They don't make much sense," he said. "In fact, they don't make any sense at all."

He was already moving back along the corridor. We followed. Looking back over his shoulder, he said: "They're like children. Moronic. Half the time I can't tell what they say. They made contact in response to the alarm, but I don't think they know what they're doing at all. I get the impression that they think it's God talking. They keep saying 'Thank God' over and over."

Nathan wouldn't look at me. I don't think he wanted to see my face.

"Something," said Pete Rolving, as we reached the radio, "is wrong."

Chapter 3

~~~~~~~~~~~~~~~~~~~~~~~~~

They couldn't give us co-ordinates to tell us where to set down. In fact, they couldn't tell us anything. They had opened a circuit, but not to communicate. As Pete had said, they had reacted to the alarm on their set. They had made the bell stop ringing. But they didn't seem to know what was going on—like very young children . . . or idiots. We could hear them talking, but not to us.

Later, in orbit, we got a fix on their signal. Pete took the ship down manually, and very carefully. We used a bit more fuel than we should have done, but it was like aiming for a postage stamp. There was a hillside, cleared of trees, where a settlement had been established. It wasn't very big, to say the least. About two miles by one and a half, including the crest of the hill and long, shallow slopes.

We settled like a feather, almost exactly in the center. We looked out, through the ship's eyes: four screens gave us a complete panoramic view.

There were houses on the slopes—a group to the south, odd ones scattered elsewhere, between fields which, once upon a time, had been marked out for grain and vegetables. The houses, so far as we could see, were in a state of some dilapidation. The nearest structure to the spot where we'd set down was a cairn of squarish stones, set right on the crown of the hill.

We didn't see the people, not immediately. They must have hidden from the noise of our backblast and the sight of our mass floating down out of the clouds. It's an intimidating sight.

While we watched, however, they began to come out.

The first ones were children, but the initiative seized by the very young was soon pre-empted by the old. It was the adults who came right up the' slope to stare at the ship from close range. There weren't many. About ten came close, there might have been sixty or seventy more watching from a distance, including all the children.

They just stared. And waited. They were thin, almost cadaverous, with the skin sticking close to their bones. Their cheeks were hollow, their eyes seemingly deep-set, large and shadowed. The garments they wore were unimaginably tattered, reduced to mere rags. And yet they retained the echoes of careful mass production. They were the remnants of garments brought to Dendra by the original colonists.

Over one hundred and fifty years before.

The original colonists had made a start. They had cleared land here—we were several thousand feet above sea level, and the trees were spaced out here, but even so a good deal of work must have gone into the preparation of the fields. They had built a village, or begun to build one. On the slope of another hill, beyond a shallow saddle, we could see where they had begun to build more houses, had begun to clear more land—a not inconsiderable tract of it. But they had failed, there. The forest had reclaimed the region, and there was a wall extending across the saddle now, cutting off the settlement from the land that had been allowed to go wild. The wall, it seemed, ran all the way round the tiny parcel of land which was all that remained of the original plan.

In a hundred and fifty years, they could have extended over a hundred hills, mile by mile, month by month. They'd had all the time in the world.

But they hadn't used it.

Instead, the forest had driven them back, enclosed them, reduced them.

Was this really all that was left? I wondered. Less than a hundred people, in decaying houses, scraping a living of appalling poverty from a handful of fields slowly turning wild?

I looked again at the small knot of people, patiently staring at the great metal edifice that had fallen from their sky. They were starving.

But why? Even if the corn had failed, even if the hens had all died, the potatoes been blighted, if everything they had brought had failed, there was plenty that was edible in the forest. Meat, fruits, roots—and perennially available, for there was no winter here. They *couldn't* starve.

And the houses which were falling down, roofs caving in, pitted walls, missing doors. Why? Were they helpless?

There was only one possible answer to that. They *were* helpless. Helpless, it seemed, to do anything but survive. And perhaps they were failing in that, too. Their faces seemed vacuous, hideous with the absence of any real sign of life or thought.

Like children, Pete had said. And some of them were. Moronic, he had said, and as to that, they *all* were. Or so it seemed. A population robbed of intelligence, robbed of knowledge, robbed of humanity.

"I'm going out," said Nathan. Nobody leapt up to volunteer to go with him.

Others were coming up the hill, now, to join the boldest. First they came in ones, and then the movement took hold of them all, and they came in a ragged crowd. A few more appeared from the houses in the huddled group.

"Is that *all* of them?" whispered Linda.

"All except the halt and the lame," I answered.

A couple of minutes passed while Nathan went through the safety lock. He appeared outside, glancing back apprehensively at the ship's eye, through which we watched him.

He walked toward the crowd. Many of them shrank back fearfully.

We weren't wired for sound. We couldn't hear what he said to them, nor what they replied. But they *did* reply. They spoke. But whatever they said didn't seem to make much sense to Nathan.

He was trying to locate a leader or a spokesman, someone who could answer questions. We watched him looking round, trying to find someone. But there was no such person. They all talked. *At* him rather than to him.

An absurd scenario unfolded in my mind. Once, it had been accepted as rational, almost inevitable. A colony on an alien planet forgets all the knowledge bequeathed to it by Earth. Its inhabitants became savages. When new men arrive from Earth, the savages take the newcomers for gods. Just as the South American Indians took the invading Europeans for gods.

They thought it was God talking, I said to myself. Out of the radio. They think Nathan is God. Come to visit them. Come to rescue them. Come to destroy them. And they don't seem to care. They haven't fallen on their knees. They aren't wailing and gnashing their teeth. They're just babbling like idiots.

Maybe, I thought, they're waiting for a miracle. Or are we miracle enough in ourselves?

"One thing's certain," said Karen. "We aren't going to spark off a revolution here. They sure as hell aren't going to think we've come to steal their promised land."

I turned to Mariel Valory.

"What do you make of it?" I asked.

If anyone could make anything of it, it had to be Mariel. She had a talent, a special understanding. Whether it was mind-reading or not no one was very sure, but she didn't need words. She could read faces.

She was staring hard at the screen, trying to see whatever there was to be seen.

"They don't understand," she said. "They just have no idea who or what we are. It's a complete mystery to them. One or two of them—the ones who came up the hill first—seem hopeful. But they don't know what to hope *for*. As an event in their lives, this is meaningless."

"They kept saying: 'Thank God,'" said Karen. "Over the radio."

"Some of them seem to be saying it now," said Mariel. "But they're just mouthing it. As if it were a formula, something to repeat over and over in moments of stress. It doesn't hold any meaning. Nothing seems to hold much meaning. It's as if they aren't really there. Not as people. Not as *minds*."

As a reading, it looked pretty good. We all got something of the same impression. These people had forgotten, all right, but they hadn't merely gone back to being savages. They'd gone back to being ghosts, shadow-people. Savages are survivors, coping with their environment effectively, albeit in a state of ignorance. These people were *not* coping. They were living very close to the survival margin—to the most critical threshold of all. The decay that was in the fields and the houses was in them, too.

Nathan signalled to the eye that he was coming back in.

When he turned around, the crowd just stared after him. They didn't protest. They didn't call after him. They didn't attempt to follow. But when he was back, they began to disperse, slowly. They thought it was over. And it hadn't even begun.

Nathan re-entered the room. His face was set like stone.

Take it as it comes, he had said. No judgments. No condemnations.

"How bad is it?" asked Conrad.

"I can't get through," said Nathan. "They speak English, they know the words I use. But the message doesn't get across. It's not just that they're stupid. They're withdrawn. Crazy. Wrapped up in themselves. It's going to be difficult."

Then his voice changed slightly, became more aggressive. "But we can do it," he went on. "We can make contact. It's going to take time and work, but we can rescue these people from whatever kind of dead end they're in. We start right away. Mariel, you come with me to the village. Conrad, you look around the houses, too. A lot of these people are physically sick, find out how many and what we have to cope with. Alex, you and Linda take a walk round the whole settlement, the fields, the edge of the forest. Get a general impression of the state of affairs, and start making guesses as to what might have happened and why."

It was no time to object to his handing out orders. He had the right idea. Start right in, without giving ourselves a chance to recoil.

Two by two, we went out through the safety lock. I came through last of all, the odd one out. The air outside was cool. There was a wind blowing from the south that cut a chill into me instantly. Three weeks in thermostatically controlled air leaves you vulnerable to a cold wind. But it wouldn't take long to adjust.

It was early morning, and the sun was just getting up to a modest height. There was some cloud about but it looked as if the weather was set fair.

All that was left of the crowd were a handful of children. They retreated before we dispersed, but continued to watch us from a respectable distance. Nathan, Mariel and Conrad set off down the slope toward the little clot of houses. I led Linda off at right angles, along the side of the hill.

Once we were clear of the ground that had been scorched by our backblast I knelt to inspect the grass. Tough Earth-type species brought to assist in claiming the land from the native forms grew in loose tussocks scattered here and there. There were Dendran grasses too. There were also potatoes, which had once enjoyed sole priority here but which now grew wild, vying with anything else the wind brought. There were other plants, too —Dendran plants which were already spreading clusters of spatulate leaves from tough, tall stalks to shade the ground, preparing the way for the return of the trees. For the forest to reclaim this land would take another forty or fifty years—two generations, in human terms—but it could be done, unless human intervention prevented it.

Between the fields marked out by the original settlers were hedges of imported thorn-bushes, but the hedge-rows had been invaded in no certain terms by native species. There were small birds nesting there, and a profusion of flowering plants dressing the fringes with colored blossoms. On most of the plants there were healthy blooms intermingled with new buds and dying inflorescences. On Dendra, the cycle of life was closed upon itself.

We made our way through the gaps in the hedges over toward the eastern edge of the settlement, toward the rough wooden fence which marked the boundary of what was now the human domain. Because we were higher up the slope we could see over the fence into the youthful forest which was already well advanced in the process of regeneration over and around the wreckage of a long-abandoned attempt to extend that domain for miles and miles in every direction. The wood that had once been felled had been translated into buildings: from Dendran forest into human farmland, complete with houses, barns, silos. And then back again.

Even in the small rectangle of land which remained, at least partly, under the domination of the extraplanetary invaders, there was no sign of domestic animals save for hens in wooden runs within the conglomerate of dwellings. Yet the forest contained creatures like pigs, flightless fowl of several native varieties, creatures like small goats, scavengers like dogs. If anything had ever been co-opted from the forest into the pattern of human life on Dendra, it had since been abandoned, sent back where it came from.

"Perhaps," said Linda, "this isn't the only settlement. Perhaps they found better places, and abandoned this." She couldn't muster any real conviction.

"And the people too?" I said. "Are the ones we find here just the abandoned and forsaken? The moronic and the insane? While elsewhere in the forest there's a Utopian community where everything is beautiful?"

I couldn't believe it. I didn't even want to believe it.

We came to the barrier which sought, impotently, to keep the forest at bay. It was taller than it had seemed from the crest of the hill. It was also more solid, at least at the point where we stood. It had been built to last, its logs tightly knitted into a solid barricade seven feet high, strengthened every ten or twelve yards by stout buttresses.

Considering its uselessness, it was surprisingly well put together.

"I don't really see the point of this," I said.

"There are predators in the forest," Linda reminded me. "Things like leopards—and scavengers, pests of one kind and another."

I shook my head. "As a means of keeping things out," I pointed out, "it's no good at all. Things which live in forests tend to be able to climb trees, and anything that could climb a tree could climb this. It's pretty solid, but there are gaps at ground level which would easily let something the size of a rat or a snake through. It's not a defensive wall, it marks the boundary. The boundary they decided to settle for, when it became clear to them that all their attempts to expand were doomed to failure."

"But *why* were they doomed to failure? They obviously cleared a lot more land than this to start with. Why couldn't they keep it clear?"

That, of course, was the big question, and we were still a long, long way from a big answer. What was bugging me, right at that moment, was a much smaller question —maybe even a silly question. Why build a boundary so big and tough? It went all around the perimeter, maybe seven miles in all. How ridiculous to put the logs which went into it to such a futile use, instead of building houses, making something *functional*. It made no sense.

"Well," I said to Linda, "this is the first time for us. Conrad's seen it before—though not quite so bad. This is what we expected, if we expected anything."

Conrad had been out with the *Daedalus* on its first recontact mission, with Kilner. They had found five colonies engaged in a desperate struggle to survive, fighting a slow losing battle. They hadn't been so far gone as this one—and, in fact, the visit of the *Daedalus* might have helped them turn the corner and start winning— but this seemed to belong to the same deadly pattern. For Linda and myself, as I'd said, it was the first time we had seen it. Floria had been an exception.

I was hoping, just then, that time wouldn't prove Floria to be *the* exception.

"It's horrible," she said. "Maybe I should have expected it—feared it. But there's just no way you can be prepared."

I nodded my complete agreement to that.

I gripped the top of the wooden wall and scrambled up by means of the abundant toeholds left by the curvature of the logs. I straddled the top while I helped Linda to get up beside me, then I swung round to sit on top of the structure. She did the same. Neither of us jumped down to set our feet on the soil that had been conceded to the alien world. We looked out at the sea of saplings and the clumps of bushes. Young forest, stretching away across the saddle between the hilltops, and up the distant slope. Beyond the crown of the hill we could see the *real* forest, in all its ancient majesty: trees a hundred feet tall even at this elevation. Down in the valleys, where the rivers ran, there would be trees like no trees which had *ever* grown on Earth. Vast and incredibly ancient.

The young forest was so *very* young. I knew as I looked at it that this was not the true Dendra but a pale shadow.

Forests, however, are very patient.

The untidy stand of saplings, with their woefully inadequate crowns of thin branches and slender leaves, lacked the dignity of age, but was full of life. There was a constant flurry of movement within the bushes as crowds of small birds hopped and fluttered from branch to branch. There seemed to be a great number of butterflies and other winged insects.

It didn't seem strange to me, as I perched on top of the wall, that the butterflies stayed outside, in Dendran territory, as did most of the birds and many of the other flying things. I sat at the junction of two worlds—different worlds. It was natural that each should possess its own native life, and should share so very little. In my head, I knew that the two worlds were not so different. Both were in the process of returning to the original state that each had enjoyed before the human colonists ever arrived. One was moving a little faster than the other, had got a little further, but *essentially* the situations were the same. My eyes, however, lied just a little, and told me that there were, indeed, two worlds.

My ears, too, confirmed the difference. The settlement land was almost silent, but the forest was a continuing chaos of whistles, clicks, creaks and rustles, as if the trees themselves were continually shuffling their feet. The youthful forest seemed to be *busy*—not merely active but *at work*. The human domain was derelict, still in the process of dying even while it was in the early stages of rebirth.

I realized that I felt slightly sick. The revelation of what was here had gone to my stomach. In my head I felt little —not even sadness. The sense of tragedy was more physical than that.

Floria had been far from perfect, the colonists had needed our help badly, but the people there had been *successful*. They had done what they had set out to do. They had had every chance to do it. Almost everything had been in their favor, and the one thing that had not had now been set aside, thanks to the *Daedalus*.

But here . . .

"No judgments," I murmured.

"What?"

I glanced at Linda, making a slight grimace. "We're supposed to ask why," I said. "But there are certain answers we're not allowed to arrive at. We're not allowed to answer that they never had a chance in the first place, that they should never have been sent."

"That's not an answer at all," she said. "That's what comes *after* the answer. It's the excuse. *An* excuse."

What she left unsaid was: 'And it *isn't* any part of our job to provide excuses.'

I hopped down off the wall, just for a moment. Linda didn't follow. I took only three or four paces away from her. I didn't reach out to touch anything. I paused, and looked back.

"It smells good," she said, looking down at me.

I realised that she was right. The one thing the survey's olfactory analyses hadn't said, and I'd almost missed it, too. Like their mechanical apparatus, my mind had been tied up with abstract matters.

It *did* smell good. I breathed in deeply. The extra two or three per cent oxygen didn't give me any lift. It wasn't enough of an increase to have an intoxicating effect.

I came back to the wall and jumped up. I scrambled over and dropped back inside. There would be other times to go into the forest, to see the alien world on its own terms. Not now.

Linda came down too, and we both looked at the wall from within, still not quite understanding why it was there.

"You're right," she said. "It is absurd. An awful lot of work has to be put into building something like that. Mile upon mile. . . ."

"I don't believe it's a physical barrier at all," I said. "I think it's a psychological one."

"That's ridiculous," she objected. "*Nobody* would build a seven mile wall for psychological reasons."

I shrugged.

"It seems to me," I replied, in a low voice, "that nobody would build one for any other kind of reasons."

Chapter 4

As night fell, making nonsense once again of the dutiful hands of the ship's clock and the schedule of shifts by which Pete and Karen, at least, tried hard to operate, we all gathered back at the ship.

On Floria, first night down, we'd been treated by the locals to an evening of celebration. By the time we'd all got together again aboard the *Daedalus* our thoughts had been turned toward the next morning. We'd had little enough to say to one another.

This first night down could hardly have been more different. We *had* to talk. We'd been pitched into a situation which seemed desperate. For the Dendran colonists this was the eleventh hour, or maybe later. Maybe *too* late. We had to talk—to attack the situation with all the intellectual artillery at our disposal.

"There are just ninety-two left," said Nathan. "Originally, there were more than fourteen hundred."

"We don't know that both ships made it," objected Linda Beck. "There could have been a disaster in ultraspace."

Nathan shook his head. "I've looked around the village, the core of the settlement. The original ships were cannibalized in order to provide the initial shelters. There are bits of both ships built into the structure of the buildings."

"Can you be sure that there are bits of *two* ships, not one?" This questions came from Pete Rolving. The point did need pressing.

"We'll take a closer look in good time," said Nathan. "But I think there are two."

"What about the people?" I asked.

Nathan looked at Conrad. Conrad deferred to Mariel. She had been sitting with her elbows on the table and her head cupped in her hands. She looked unhappy, but she sat up straight.

"A few years ago," she said, "they tried to use my talent in psychiatry. I was only ten . . . eleven . . . it lasted six months or so. The idea was that I could get inside people's problems, find out why they were *really* screwed up, instead of why they *thought* they were. It worked, after a fashion. But I didn't like it. I didn't have much contact with extreme psychosis—usually it was personal problems, depression, dislocation. Crazy people—*really* crazy people—made me sick. My father, and some of the doctors, thought I was in danger. The whole thing never really got off the ground. They tried to teach me some theory, but I was too young. I didn't get it. And it didn't seem to fit with the kind of thing I read anyhow.

"What I'm trying to lead up to is this. Those people aren't just simple. They're mad. They're sick."

"They're schizoid," said Conrad, cutting in quickly. "Dislocated from their surroundings. Out of contact with the environment. But it's something that's arisen quite naturally out of the way they're living. They haven't 'gone insane.' They're not psychotic. I don't believe there's any physical damage to their brains. It's a matter of the way they've grown up, in a depleted environment. Not only physically depleted but mentally. They talk, but they don't really communicate. They're living half-lives, having lost virtually everything the original colonists had: all the knowledge, all the values, the sense of identity. Their humanity has simply drained away, over the years and the generations. They retain enough to survive—just. The population is imbalanced, incidentally there are twice as many females as males, and the ratio is much higher in the higher age-groups. It seems the women cope better than the men, or the girls than the boys."

"Can we get through to them?" asked Linda.

"In time," said Nathan. Mariel confirmed what he said with a nod. "Especially the children," he went on. "They may be the ones to concentrate on. They can learn. They can be re-educated."

"And then?" I said.

Nathan looked at me, and waited.

"What are we going to try to do?" I said. "You say they can be re-educated, but what's the aim of the re-education? To turn them back into decent human beings, like the original colonists? To wind them up like clockwork toys, and then to let them go so they can repeat the whole process? There are *less than a hundred!* If fourteen hundred able and knowledgeable people couldn't cope, couldn't *begin* to build a viable colony here, what chance have ninety-two?"

"That depends," said Nathan coolly.

"On what?"

"On what prevented the original colonists from carrying through what they started. On whether we can find out what it was. And on what we can do about seeing that it doesn't happen again."

"You talk as if the colony had been the victim of some kind of disaster," I said. "Something that could have been avoided if it could have been foreseen. We don't know that."

"We don't know anything, yet," he countered. "We have to find out. And while we're finding out, we have to do what we can. There are no alternatives, Alex. We have to do what we can to help these people survive here. We can't take them away."

"No," I said, harshly. "We can't." I shut up, then. There was no point in going on.

Nathan was quick to move in the falling silence. "There are a few other points which ought to be mentioned," he said. "Concerning what I saw in the village. I saw the radio, which is still, as we know, operative. There's other equipment from the ships. But what I *didn't* see is any sign of the data bank: the tapes, the films, the equipment for use with the tapes and films. That's something we'll have to search for, if we're going to discover why all the knowledge contained in that bank no longer exists—or *seems* not to exist—in the minds of the people.

"The people seem to live exclusively out of what remains of the original farming operation. They have chickens, eggs, and vegetables still growing in the fields. I saw no sign of anything gathered from the forest.

"Another thing I didn't find was a graveyard. If the

original colonists had put up commemorative markers—or any sort of markers at all—we might have a better idea of the pattern of decline. But it seems the dead are simply buried. No records. No memories. In fact, the generations that have passed away seem to have left very little of themselves behind at all. So little that I wonder if maybe they didn't go somewhere else."

"You think what's left is only a remnant of the original colony?" asked Karen. "That the rest are living elsewhere."

"Maybe not living," said Nathan. "Perhaps they went elsewhere and died."

"Into the forest?" This from Linda.

"And that," I mused, chipping in again, "might explain the wall. It might explain why the present generation are so afraid of the forest, if something out there killed a large number of the original settlers."

It made a kind of sense. The survey team had spent a year in the forest and found nothing inimical. But the settlers were here for a lifetime—all the time in the world to find what the survey team had missed.

"The present settlers," said Conrad, quietly, "don't seem to know *why* they fear the forest. We couldn't get any answers. It's all very well to suggest that something in the forest kills people, but it doesn't begin to explain what's happened *here*, inside the settlement."

And that was true enough, too.

"The people out there *now*," said Conrad, continuing in the same calm tone, "are the sixth and seventh generations. But the sixth generation must have overlapped the fourth, and the fourth the second. It's not a long chain of communication. The kind of mental deterioration which has happened here wasn't caused by simple forgetfulness. A generation doesn't grow up in this kind of total ignorance unless something happened to prevent one of the prior generations passing on what they knew.

"Before the *Daedalus* set out on its first tour we discussed the possibility of historical regression in the colonies. It seemed a real possibility that the descendants of the actual settlers might grow up to learn a wholly different scheme of things, without most of the knowledge their parents needed and took for granted. But the colonists who came out here, and to all the other worlds, knew the danger of concentrating exclusively on practical matters. They knew how vital it was to protect the information they carried with them, how necessary it was to make *use* of it in every way possible. They must have had plans to guard that heritage as the most precious thing they brought with them from Earth, for that is what it was.

"These people here have lost that heritage, and it isn't a trivial question to ask how. Indeed, it's the most important question of all, especially in view of what Nathan has said about there being no sign of the data bank or its associated equipment in the village. If it isn't there, *where is it?*"

No one had anything to add to that.

"You've been through those survey reports more often than anyone, Alex," said Nathan. "Now you've had your twenty minutes on the ground, too. Do you have anything to add?"

I regretted my cavalier statement about being able to deduce more from twenty minutes direct observation than from weeks of careful study. All I really had to add was the fact that the forest had a pleasant smell.

"There were once fourteen hundred people here," I said, recapitulating the basics while I fought to see some significant possibility hitherto overlooked. "That was a century and a half ago. They started to clear land, to build houses. And they mde a good start. They *did* clear land—more than this tiny area—and they did build houses. They planned fields, built hedges, planted crops.

"But then, some time later, they changed their priorities. They retreated to a pitiful tract of land barely three square miles in area. They walled it in and surrendered the land outside. To judge by the extent to which the forest has reclaimed that land I'd guess this happened a hundred years ago, give or take fifteen.

"Something happened to change their minds. Not necessarily something sudden. A growing realization that they couldn't make it—a gradual acceptance of defeat—could have forced the decision just as easily as any specific catastrophe. But when they retreated, they retreated all the way. Not just physically, but in terms of what they were trying to do. Their original intention must have been to select what was useful from the native land and combine it with what they had brought with them, to achieve a synthesis of the two life-systems which would permit them to live and grow. For some reason, they discovered —or concluded—that such a synthesis was either impossible or undesirable.

"The obvious explanation is that they discovered something in the native life-system inimical to human life. The survey team found nothing, but that's not necessarily conclusive. The team that surveyed Floria didn't identify the tricky factor there. We must also presume that whatever they found is responsible for the mental breakdown of the colonists after or during the period of retreat.

"That's the obvious explanation. In skeletal form, at least. I can't think, off-hand, of a respectable alternative. But I don't feel happy about it. There's something missing. Not just a detail, but something major. An extra factor."

"Why so sure?" asked Linda.

They were all waiting for some amazing relevation. I didn't have one. All I had was a feeling.

"The wall," I said. "It doesn't keep the forest out. It keeps the people in. Their rejection of the forest is more than just the result of finding danger there. Psychologically, it's more powerful than that. And more subtle. Hatred, rather than fear. That wall is a gesture of defiance, not a barrier."

I stopped, losing the thread of the thought. I didn't seem to have got anywhere. I looked up, at the circle of faces, still expectant.

"Whatever the answer is," I said. "We won't find it here. We'll have to look for it in the forest."

And we all knew who was going to be the one who went looking.

Chapter 5

The next two days passed slowly. It was the kind of time interval which tends to become marginal when relegated to the memory, as though of doubtful reality. I do not remember the days as patterns of events but as one deep well of emotional reaction from which I was eager to be released. The quality of the emotion involved was not easy to label. It lasted too long to be called *horror*. It was more a kind of psychological nausea.

The village was a village of ghosts. The houses, despite their tenants, were locked into the process of slow deterioration which one associates with total neglect: erosion by weather and waste. Of the people, some talked hardly at all, and others hardly stopped, but the latter exercised little control over the constant spillage of phonemic assemblies which no longer encoded concious ideas by any effort of will.

They were docile. They accepted whatever we tried to do to and for them with a fatalism barely touched by fear. The children tended to follow us around, to watch what we did with wide-eyed stares still, apparently, possessed of a glimmering curiosity.

The situation was by no means hopeless. The total lack of any real animal aggression—which had, no doubt, been a contributory factor in the general decay—would work in our favor while we attempted to re-educate the relict of the colony. Nathan, at least, was outwardly confident that we could salvage the minds of the younger members of the population. There was no possibility of turning them into beings like ourselves, but we could show them ways to survive more easily, and perhaps reinvest them with the will to do so. But setting them up again was the lesser part of the problem. The greater part lay in trying to discover why the disaster had occurred in the first place, and in asking the question of whether it might not happen yet again.

As we went among the people in the settlement in those two days we found ourselves acting a part—a part for which none of us was entirely suited. They did not seek to make gods out of us, and we did not want to pretend to such a role, but the situation was shaped in such a way that the prerogatives normally abandoned to god or chance became ours. We had to make decisions about the way in which the lives of the people were to be redesigned and redirected. It was a responsibility that I, for one, did not find comfortable.

Conrad, Linda and I spent the two days conducting medical examinations with all the thoroughness and analytical sophistication at the disposal of the *Daedalus* lab. We found the colonists to be suffering from various deficiency diseases and general malnutrition, but none of the serious organic malfunctions which prey upon people so weakened on Earth. Dendra, in fact, was a remarkably healthy place to live. Although there were mammalian creatures in the native life-system their bodily chemistry was sufficiently different to set up a considerable barrier to bacterial and virus adaptation. The original colonists, of course, had been rigorously debugged in order to prevent their importing anything potentially dangerous. The people of the settlement were having a little trouble with plant ectoparasites, fungal skin-infections, but internally they were virtually free of toxic infection. Nearly all of them, of course, would have developed allergy reactions to local proteins, but local circumstances generally permitted no build-up of allergens in the local environment, thus preventing the massive reactions often associated with pollen seasons on Earth. Although the survey team had found the air to be replete with strange substances their concentration was always well below danger level. The unusual steadiness of the atmospheric circulation—the wind which blew perpetually from the south—helped maintain this constancy.

While my team did the initial work required to begin

the work of bringing the people back to a state of
bodily health Nathan, assisted by Mariel and occasionally
Karen, mounted his own program of investigation. They
made little progress in trying to get information from the
people and came to pin their hopes more on the collection of indirect evidence. They began to mount compre-
hensive searches of the old buildings, especially the ones
in the village itself, which had presumably been more
than just dwellings.

They confirmed without much trouble that both ships
had, in fact, reached Dendra. The empty shells of those
ships contributed the structural frameworks for virtually
all the oldest edifices. All the tools and implements possessed and used by the colonists had been improvised from
the cannibalized ships. Many of those tools were still
around, having seen relatively little use in the intervening
years. Some of the fuel cells still carried a full charge.
This was understandable with respect to the cell powering
the radio, but it seemed incredible that so little of the
meager supply of available power given to the original
colonists had been used. It seemed that the legacy of
Earth—poor enough as it was—had been unappreciated.

One particular fraction of that legacy—the most important part of all—was missing altogether. The searches
turned up not the least sign of the massive library that
the colonists had brought with them, the wealth of
knowledge which was the most significant wealth the
colony could hope to possess for many generations.

All in all, the situation was tragic, and mysterious. The
original colonists had come more than a hundred light-
years in search of a new world and a new life, not
only for themselves but also, and primarily, for their
children and their children's children. And it had all gone
to waste. They had not only failed but had, it seemed,
left no explanation of their failure. They had bequeathed
to the few survivors of the potential host of their children's children only the ruins of what they had brought
from Earth. Pitiful ruins. They had not managed to
make anything that belonged to the forest a part of the
life they handed down. Their legacy contained neither a
pattern for survival nor even a *will* to survive. Had the
Daedalus arrived twenty or forty years later, we might
well have found nothing but bones.

How could they have let it happen? I asked myself, many times. How could they have failed so completely?

The people in the settlement were victims, and the more I found out about them the more it seemed to me that they were victims not of chance or alien circumstances but of their own ancestors, who had, even if only by default, delivered them into their present desolation. They had not "regressed" into listless barbarity, but had been abandoned to it.

It was not until the evening of the second day that we managed to turn up a significant, or apparently-significant, piece of evidence relating to the early colonists.

It was a book. It was hand-made. Some books, printed on imperishable plastic, would have been among the stored information brought out from Earth, but books are, for the most part, a little too bulky to recommend themselves for expensive spacelift. As a distribution-system rather than a storage-system, however, books are extremely useful and books are one of the items one looks to find on the priority list of artifacts to be manufactured *in situ* by a new colony. The content of such books may be expected to reflect the primary concerns and ambitions of the colonists.

The book which Nathan found was about the forest. The forest had apparently contributed significantly to its make-up, for it was bound in bark and appeared to have been sewn and glued with native materials. Only the pages, sewn in one by one, had been recovered from materials taken from the ships. The book had suffered over the years, but was internally sound and the hand-written pages could still be read.

The book was a guide, not to replace, but rather to supplement, the survey reports which must have been the handbook to survival used by the settlers. Although a considerable amount of work had gone into it, it was not an *end*-product so much as a work perpetually *in progress*, being steadily extended, improved and revised. It had numerous illustrations, some hand-colored with inks of presumably local origin. As a commentary it was practical in tone and style. Unlike the survey reports, which classified things as edible or inedible, with precise analyses of nutritional value, the book classified things as pleasant or unpleasant to eat, with recommendations as

to cooking and preparation. Where the survey reports
described a certain kind of cat-like predator the book
provided an illustration with the comment in capi-
tals: THIS ANIMAL IS DANGEROUS. And so on.

Rough-and-ready though it was, the book must have
been the central reservoir of the information collected by
the original colonists during their constructive years. It
was difficult to estimate how much time had gone into the
assembly of the information it contained, primarily because we could not estimate the number of contributors.
In the six hundred and some pages we could detect at
least twenty different hands, but how many minds had
supplied the hands with information we could not guess.

I spent the second night reading the book and trying
to digest its content. I was allowed to monopolize it
primarily because I was the one who would have to make
use of the information when I went into the forest.

The one thing the book did not contain was any historical or journalistic material on the colony itself. Nor
was there any internal evidence to suggest why the book
had been abandoned. No one had written an epilogue, nor
so much as a single bitter footnote to hint at the reasons
for the death of everything it represented. It seemed that
whatever disaster had come had struck suddenly and without foreboding, like lightning from a clear sky.

Or had it?

"The strangest thing of all," I said, "is that we should
have found this one book, all alone. Where are the others,
and why is this not with them?"

The question was addressed to Nathan, in the early
hours of the morning of the third day. The only other
member of the party present was Pete Rolving, who was
still operating on the ship's clock despite the fact that
eight-hourly watches and systems checks were no longer
required. Work on the ship invariably seemed to expand
to fill as much time as Pete could find to make available
for it.

"The library isn't here," said Nathan. "I wasn't sure of
that before, but I am now. It would be too big to hide so
effectively that our search could have missed it. And if
it isn't here that implies that it was either destroyed or
removed."

"All except for this one," I repeated.

Nathan looked at it. It lay open on the table in front of me, and his eyes ran over the lines of spidery handwriting, studded with marginal notes and blotches where statements had been erased after due consideration.

"If the colonists moved on elsewhere," I said. "This is the one book that they absolutely would not leave behind. Not if they were going to carry all the rest with them."

"Mightn't it also be the one book that they'd hold back from destruction?" he asked, trying the idea out for size.

"Why would they destroy everything else?" I asked, raising the obvious objection. "Including the survey reports to which this is really only a sequel?"

"True," he admitted, and went on without pause to new possibilities. "Then suppose, instead, that only *some* of the colonists left. Suppose the colony split into two— half staying here, half seeking fresh pastures. Suppose that they decided to divide up the assets. The ones who went away couldn't carry the bodywork of the ships, or the cleared land, or the standing buildings, so they took as their share what was portable, or they tried. And in the bargaining, the ones who stayed claimed *this*."

Before I could raise the three hundred obvious objections to this theory, Pete chipped in.

"Suppose," he said, "that there were duplicate copies. Then, wherever the library is, there could be this too. You don't have to make out a special case for it then."

"That's a possibility," I said. "If they had the materials available, it would make sense to keep vital information like this in duplicate. But the whole notion of the colony splitting in two is absurd. How could that possibly be in anyone's interest. To halve the legacy would leave no one with a sufficiency."

"You're right," said Nathan. "It *is* absurd. But it isn't impossible. And what's more, absurdity isn't necessarily the same thing as implausibility. Not when you're dealing with the behavior of humans—especially humans in groups."

I must have looked at him with open-mouthed astonishment. But I also thought about what he had said. Somehow, it didn't seem as unlikely as all that. I *could* imagine it happening. Internecine strife, violent disagreements and arguments forcing more and more commitment, more and more extremism and polarization of ideas. A small community, unable to get along as a single corporate entity, splitting into two . . .

. . . and dividing up all that they possessed, leaving neither fraction with the necessities of life?

It was absurd. But was it believable?

Was it more believable, for instance, than the idea that someone had taken it upon himself to destroy, obliterating without trace, the whole data bank brought by the colonists from Earth? Or the hypothesis that some inconceivable event had somehow resulted in the accidental destruction of everything but the one remaining book, and had simultaneously destroyed all the chances the colonists had ever had of establishing themselves in this tiny area?

I reached out with my hands, and closed the book, closing, as I did so, the discussion of the issues which had been raised. There seemed no point in continuing, as we were already hopelessly lost in imaginative realms so remote from probability.

"The whole situation," I said, "is threatening to drive me out of my mind."

"Mmmm," said Nathan, pensively. "That's something else I felt I ought to mention." There was a new note in his voice. A note of anxiety.

"How do you mean?" I said, not understanding.

"If you cast your mind back," he said, "to the very beginning of the affair on Floria, you may remember something you said to me about Mariel. You said that you were set against the idea of her being sent on this expedition, because, for one thing, you didn't believe she could use her talent to deal with aliens, and for another, because you thought it might just make her receptive enough to alien minds to drive her out of her own."

"I remember," I said.

"Well, I've been thinking about it. Whether you're right about the aliens, I don't know. No one really knows how Mariel's talent works. I guess we'll find out whether she's useful or not next year, on the first colony we visit where there are intelligent indigenes. But in the meantime these people here are sick, Alex. For whatever reason, their heads aren't straight. You heard what Mariel had to say about the difficulties of trying to work with disturbed minds, and quite frankly, I think she understated the case.

"I think the people here are having a bad effect on her, Alex. She's trying hard to make contact with them— to open lines of communication. And I think she's trying too hard. I'm not sure if it's a good thing to have her empathizing with people who are mentally ill. I think there's a very real danger to her—a danger of infection."

I let the idea sink in. "I don't know," I said. "To me, she always seems . . . uncomfortable. I don't talk to her much. And I don't really know much about her talent. She told me that it was simply intuitive non-verbal communication —being able to read in face muscles what isn't said in words."

"That's part of it," said Nathan, "but not the whole. Doctors trying to analyze her ability have said that—have told her that—but they were the sort of men who went looking for a simple explanation, determined to find one. Any explanation was better than none—you know how some scientists try to minimize events rather than accepting their own ignorance. It's a rebellion against the kind of supernatural explanations people are all too ready to invent where scientists can't provide an immediate answer. Yes, there's a certain degree of simple non-verbal communication involved. But there's also *complex* non-verbal communication. I don't want to use the word *telepathy* or the manifold vulgarizations of it. But Mariel *can* empathize with people to an extraordinary degree, and I think that in this particular case she could get hurt doing it. People in her kind of mental situation live, inevitably, in a schizoid world. It's not uncommon for them to become schizophrenic."

"Especially," I said, "if they're forced to live and work with schizophrenics. A whole community of them."

He nodded.

"You could be right," I affirmed. "But what can we do about it? Lock her up for the duration?"

"I want you to take her with you," he said. "Into the forest. Away from here. For a while. It's a temporary solution, but it gives us time to think."

I didn't like the idea, and I didn't bother to pretend that I did. I was uneasy in Mariel's presence. The idea that she knew more about what was going on in my mind than I chose to let out of normal channels *made* me uneasy. It wasn't that I had anything to hide, but just the simple fact—the idea of being perennially open to invasion.

"I intended to go alone," I said.

"I'd advise against that anyhow," said Nathan. "It may be dangerous out there. You know as well as I do that it would be unwise."

"I can't take Conrad or Linda," I said. "They have too much to do here. It's not just a matter of getting the people healthy, it's a matter of getting the fields healthy, reestablishing a base for adequate survival and expansion. I feel bad enough myself about turning my back on the real, obvious work for the business of simple exploring, without even knowing what I'm looking for."

"The answer, as you said, is in the forest," he reminded me.

"Sure," I said. "But the forest covers the whole world. Where do I start looking? Do I just wander round waiting for inspiration? That seems to be all there is. But I can't take half the strength away from the immediate task, now can I?"

"You can't take Conrad or Linda," agreed Nathan. "And my job is definitely here. But I think it would be as well if you took Mariel, for her own protection. And I think Karen should go with you, too. Not to help you find any answers to awkward questions, but as insurance against the possibility of something going wrong."

"Pete won't relish being left to look after the ship on his own," I said.

"The regulation about keeping two people on board at all times is a precautionary measure," Nathan pointed out. "In a sense, it's exactly the same precaution you should take. We can stick to it. Conrad and Linda will have to do more work in the lab than out there, and if we break it once in a while the sky won't fall. This isn't Floria— we know we have nothing to fear so far as threats to the hardware are concerned."

What he was saying was sensible enough. It was tempting fate to go into the forest alone. And maybe it was important to get Mariel out of the firing line. As long as Karen came too, I supposed that I could cope with my uneasiness with respect to the girl. Nathan had obviously thought it all out in advance.

"She's going to know," I pointed out. "When we tell her. She's going to know what we're going and why."

"The thing I worry about," said Nathan, "is whether we know what we're doing, and why. I'm sure of myself, but not of you. You don't help her much, you know. You avoid her. You dislike her."

"Not personally," I said. "I can't help my prejudice about the mind-reading. Maybe if I stayed here, and Conrad investigated the forest...."

"That's not an answer," he said.

I had to admit that it wasn't.

"Fair enough," I conceded. "We'll do it your way."

"Get some sleep," he advised. "There's no point in trying to commit the book to memory. You can take it out with you. But I think you should start drawing equipment when you wake up. Make a start when you can. If the forest is where the answer can be found, we need it as soon as humanly possible. Otherwise everything we do here, or try to do, might turn out to be meaningless."

I couldn't resist it. I'd spent two days and three nights not saying it.

"This world should never have been colonized," I said, as I got up, heading for my bunk. "Those people out there are all that's left of a noble experiment in political chicanery. You know that, don't you?"

His face slipped into a noncommittal mask.

"Don't start looking for the answers you *want* to find, Alex," he said. "If you do, you might find no answers at all. And even when we know the full story, even then *it's not for you to judge*. It's not for any of us."

"On the contrary," I said. "It's for each and every one of us. *Everybody* must judge."

Chapter 6

~~~~~~

The settlement's supply of fresh water was a small stream which cut diagonally across the corner that was furthest down the slope. One of the endpapers of the guidebook Nathan had found was a map, which showed that the stream wound its way on through the clustered hills to a valley where it joined a river of some magnitude. The river ran away to the north in a series of long sinuous curves, into the sub-tropical zone rather than toward the southern ocean.

The map plotted the river's course over something more than a hundred miles—five or six days' journey on foot—and ended with a rather tentative circle representing a lake. The course of the river lay between two great ridges and I hazarded a guess that the lower portion of the map had been constructed on the basis of what could be seen from the top of the higher ridge.

It seemed logical enough to follow the river ourselves when we began our trek into the forest. It would enable us to make what use there was to be made of the map, and we would presumably be retracing the steps not only of Dendra's first human explorers, but perhaps of Dendra's first mass exodus. If the colony *had* split in two—which still seemed to me to be highly unlikely—then the men who had left would almost certainly have gone north. To the south there was a relatively inhospitable mountain range and then a long drop into colder regions, while to the north there appeared to be vast plains of temperate climate and good soil.

We elected to travel as light as was practical, the only

really heavy items being the tent and a bulky power pack to supply both light and heat. In accordance with UN recommendations we took only one substantial weapon—a rather clumsy rifle equipped to carry three different clips of ammunition, two of which consisted of anaesthetic darts of varying strength and only one of which actually held lethal missiles. In the interests of self-protective convenience, however, we also carried small handguns with parabolic reflectors instead of barrels. When fired they emitted a loud bang and a brilliant flash—intimidating enough to scare away any unwelcome visitors, and even to blind them momentarily. These, like the rest of the necessary equipment—the radio, a portable lamp and the medical kit—were conveniently light.

The most precious thing we carried was the book.

When we left, the usual half-dozen children followed us across the fields and watched us climb over the wall. We had to climb—there was, in fact, no gate. Their expressions of patient wonder changed hardly at all as they watched us go. But they didn't come to the wall so that they could watch us move through the scrub to the green curtain where the foliage of the ancient forest dipped close to the ground. The wall, to them, was a conceptual barrier as well as a physical one. Once beyond it we were out of their world.

I waved to them from the top of the wall, before dropping out of sight. Surprisingly, one of them waved back. It was an oddly reassuring gesture.

We crossed the area where the forest was regenerating with some difficulty, for the ground had been left very uneven by the retreating colonists, littered with dead wood and some stones quarried from a cliff face a couple of miles away. Stiff-stemmed plants like bracken concealed much of the unevenness, and it was by no means easy to force a way through it. But the pseudo-bracken had a role to play only in the juvenile forest, and once we were into the forest proper the going became much easier. The tree trunks were much more widely spaced, and the ground between them was carpeted with plants which were not so tough and did not grow so high.

Small birds fluttered out of our way but showed no specific fear of us. They were content simply to stay out of reach. There did not seem to be so very many at a cursory glance, but our ears told us the truth which was veiled from our eyes—that there was, in fact, a great multitude hidden by the green ocean of the forest canopy. The trees, even here, grew between fifty and a hundred feet tall, and the boles of the most ancient specimens, knotted and gnarled, must have boasted a girth of thirty feet or so. Each tree extended its branches so as to barely touch the branches of one or two of its neighbors, so that sunlight crept down to the forest floor only through the strangely curved slits that remained. For the most part the lowest branches were eight or nine feet from the ground, but were virtually denuded of leaves save at their extremities. Nevertheless, the crown of each tree was a forest in its own right, on a tiny scale, hiding and sheltering birds, and perhaps beasts as well. The bark of every tree was covered by a waxy substance, which seemed lighter in color and softer in texture on the lesser trees, but blackened and set as hard as adamant on the oldest. This substance was fireproof, and though the internal wood of the trees burned well enough, forest fires could not spread on Dendra.

Because of this waxen coat, which often seemed so slick as to be polished, the insects moving on the tree trunks tended to be rather obvious. Some of them attempted to counterfeit the appearance of the wax in their own external aspect, but for the most part the legion of small flying and creeping things went in for' flamboyant dress rather than cryptic coloration. Large beetles with wing cases decorated with gaudy patterns of brilliant blue and yellow were common, and even smaller bugs with bodies little bigger than pinheads often boasted such violent crimson coloring that they looked, when massed, like countless drops of blood. The most striking members of the forest population, however, were the butterflies. On Earth, the term "butterfly" refers to a relatively small range of genera which are all anatomically similar even if their wing patterns often vary strikingly. Other, closely related, creatures we call moths. There are, however, difficulties in re-applying Earthly terminology to alien life systems, and you always find some instances where the transfer is inadequate. Dendra's butterflies were one.

In stark constrast to Floria, where nothing flew at all,

Drendra went in for flying creatures on a big scale. In a forest, this is not so surprising, especially a forest covering a whole world. The same modes of flying that had been developed on Earth had been developed here, but insect flight—and especially that variety of it practiced on Earth by butterflies and moths—had been much more heavily exploited by the evolutionary pattern. Instead of a few closely related genera the term 'butterfly,' on Dendra, had to do for a great range of quite distinct families. The differences, of course, were largely to be observed in the type of body to which the paired, colored wings were attached. Some of the insects had bulbous, colored bodies, some had hardly any bodies at all, some resembled Earthly butterflies while still others boasted amazingly complex jointed structures, waxen in texture, which were equipped with tentacular limbs. Many had no legs whatsoever, and a significant fraction were eyeless.

It can be argued that for such a profusion of types, the one term is hopelessly inadequate, but the only way to be able to speak of alien life forms at all is to co-opt the vulgar, general terms in use in common parlance and apply them where they can be made to seem appropriate. Even on Earth, such commonplace nomenclature is far from scientifically exact, so the ineptitude of the method is not really an argument against it. Trouble arises where common Earthly names are generally applied only to one species or a similar group of species—thus it is easier to use words like *butterfly, insect, mammal* and *crab* than it is to use *lion, elephant,* or even *goat*—but for the most part one can acquire a comfortable descriptive power over an alien life system by the judiciously casual redeployment of terms. Thus, the hosts of Dendra's population of multicolored flyers became butterflies, although in themselves, and by scientific standards, they were so much more.

The forest would have been beautiful without the butterflies, but it was the butterflies which really gave that beauty an obviously unearthly quality. They were everywhere, and at a casual glance you could get the idea that they were all unique, every one an individual living gem with its own particular artwork. The colors were often harsh, and the patterns lacked subtlety—bold stripes, blotches and heavy borders were as common, if not more so, as detailed, exactly-planned color schemes—but the effect of the collective phenomenon was dazzling, and, to my mind, quite superb.

The birds which we saw were mostly small, and the great majority of them, like the butterflies, were brilliantly and profusely colored. It was difficult to estimate by the evidence of the eye how many species there were in the vicinity, but our ears assured us of the diversity. Though the foliage hid large numbers from sight it was no barrier to sound. The pitch and complexity of the calls sounded by the birds was similarly multifarious. I could not honestly say that the total effect was musical. Individual songs might be tuneful and pleasant, but in the competition to be heard there were a great many notes that were harsh and strident.

We saw no more than the merest glance of creatures that were furred rather than feathered. That mammals were present in some abundance I did not doubt, but they made far more use of the cover offered by the vegetation. We caught glimpses of squirrel-like animals ducking out of sight among the branches, and there were droppings on the ground testifying to the fact that the trail we used was in constant use by other beasts which might range in size from the dimensions of a rabbit to the bulk of a pig. In actual fact creatures distinctly similar to the wild pigs of Earthly forests were just about the largest mammals on Dendra. They were omnivorous and undoubtedly used to having their own way but were—according to the colony's guide-book—not inclined to attack people. The most aggressive predators in this particular locale, according to both the survey reports and the book, were a group of species resembling medium-sized members of the Earthly cat family. The whole group had been dubbed "panthers" for convenience, although most were blotchy brown in color.

I was surprised, as we went into the deeper and more luxuriant forest in the valleys, that there still remained a good deal of light by which to see what was going on around us. Evergreen forests on Earth—especially monocultural stands—tend to be dark and gloomy, and the forests of Floria had been designed with such economical perfection that their paths were all but pitch dark. Drendra's forest was, however, more varied and more relaxed. The trees were comfortably spaced and their shapes were elegantly irrational. Most seemed to be very old indeed. The trunks varied in color from a brown so light as to be almost ochreous yellow to a deep blue-black. Most were streaked or mottled, often with metallic colors—copper and gilt. Because of the waxy tegument it often seemed that with the aid of a polishing rag a dedicated workman could make each tree gleam and shine like a vast, ornate living crystal.

The soil was moist and soft, thick with humus and scattered with loose grass and hummocks of moss or fungus. Flowering plants were common, but did not grow so profusely as to invite comparison with the birds and the insects. They were virtually all insect-pollinated and boasted blooms sculptured into all kinds of complex shapes, but for the most part they did not go in for riotous color. The pastel yellows and pinks seemed distinctly conservative by the standards set among the gaudy flying creatures. They attracted pollinators, it seemed, largely by scent. Sensory priorities were different here.

I guessed that a good many of the eyeless butterflies lived very largely by their sense of smell, experiencing the world as an ocean of organic traces. Some of the larger species might use sonar to guide them, but not the smaller ones. When you're tiny it doesn't matter much if you fly into a solid object, because you fly so slowly and the energy of collision is so very slight. Despite the fact that our superior eyesight made it easy enough to see our way in the forest the intensity of the light was such that evolution had favored different abilities in the species which had evolved to occupy this environment. I wondered whether the population of the forest underwent a considerable change after dark, with the birds resting and the bats emerging.

The air was humid and it seemed rather warmer within the forest than it had on the bare hillside of the settlement. Even the tree trunks seemed warm to the touch and it occurred to me that a certain amount of metabolic heat probably was being generated there. Down here, half-enclosed by the network of leaves and branches, was an environment so still and stable that it must be amenable to a degree of control. The survey team had commented on the constancy of the temperature in the forest and the narrow range of humidity. The forest had been here for millions of years, undisturbed save for movements of the ground itself. The whole system was integrated, and the whole environment under a form of collective homeostatic control. The forest was in many ways like a vast organism—a warm-blooded organism maintaining its own optimum internal environment.

Could it possibly be, I wondered, that the colony had failed to co-opt Dendran species to their own use because outside of their inordinately complex collectivity the organisms did not thrive? Or, even worse, underwent certain changes affecting their chemical makeup? Under different circumstances, I would have looked at the idea long and hard, but for that particular moment I filed it away. There was no time for dogmatic thinking. There was so much to see—so much that demanded the attention of my eyes and my mind.

But it was an idea I would have to return to.

Chapter 7

We made rather less progress in the morning than we might have, bearing in mind that the going was easy. We were forever pausing to look at plants, to watch butterflies, to look up into the trees at shy birds and their nests, to stir at thickets where creatures might be hiding, in pursuit of faint rustles we never quite traced to living sources. All this was, of course, primarily my fault, but neither Karen nor Mariel made any objection. They did not seem irritated, being eager enough to look themselves. Their interest was purely aesthetic, without any ulterior scientific motives, but there was a great deal for them to enjoy.

By midday I felt slightly heady. I didn't know whether to attribute it to the oxygen in the atmosphere, the organic traces in the air, or a purely subjective elation brought on by the surroundings. I guessed that all three might be true to a degree, but that the last was probably the most important. Feeling elated isn't usually a straight physiological reaction to chemicals in the environment. Feeling is something that happens in the mind, with or without the body's instigation.

I felt intoxicated because this was what it was all *about,* for me. This was what I'd come out to the stars *for.* Alien life, on its own terms, the product of alien processes; whole new worlds of living things, shaped by evolution to explore the same possibilities according to a new pattern; living things which the words I'd brought from Earth could never quite describe or conquer, needing a whole new universe of thought to understand. That's what it was all about. Up on high among the myriad fluttering wings of the colored insects were the fluttering wings of my imagination. And that was where they belonged.

It wasn't, of course, a perfect Garden of Eden. It had snakes a-plenty, although I hadn't seen one yet. Some of the insects were bothersome. None were adapted for feeding on human blood but some adventurous types were willing to have a go, and many secreted corrosive or irritant substances when touched. We accumulated our fair share of minor skin complaints as we marched, and though our medical resources were easily up to coping we couldn't quite overcome all the little trials and tribulations.

But there *are* no Gardens of Eden this side of the grave, and no one expects them. We took the forest as it came, snakes and all. It would take far more than a few minor drawbacks to destroy the fact that in opening up the colony worlds the starship had restored to humanity the whole vast concept-space of Utopian dreams. Even the failed colonies couldn't detract from the infinite possibilities, the infinite potential, that star travel had opened up for humankind.

The stream which we followed flowed slowly. It was

surprisingly deep, for although it was generally no more than a foot or two wide I couldn't find the bottom with a branch nearly as long as my leg. I judged that the rock beneath the soil must be soft, and that the water had, over the ages, hollowed out a considerable groove.

We rested when we finally reached the river into which the stream flowed. By then it was mid-afternoon. The river, too, was placid and sluggish. The lower branches of the trees leaned over its banks and sometimes trailed the tips of their leaves upon the surface. There were occasional rafts of weed—wide, lobed leaves and bowl-shaped floating blossoms like yellow water lilies. There were no crocodiles, but as we arrived I saw a couple of small darting lizards scampering over the rafts toward the bank, seeming to run on the water where necessary. There were legions of tiny frogs, green and yellow, clinging to the rafts and sitting on the bank close to the spot where we set down our packs. Unlike the more excitable creatures the frogs ignored us, remaining aloof and unintimidated.

I stood by the edge and reached out with the branch which I had been using as a staff to touch and stir things of interest, and dragged its tip through the water, sending large ripples surging out toward the rafts.

I looked up at the tall trees. Their topmost branches were driven by a steady, strong wind, and all the trees seemed to have grown to accommodate the wind. Their ultimate growing points were directed not at the zenith but almost parallel to the ground, like flags waving in the violent airstream. And yet there was hardly a breath of breeze down here, at the surface of the river.

I realized that the wind in the treetops made a curious sound: a soft susurrus like the sound of blood in human veins magnified a thousand times. As a noise it was not noticeable, drowned out by the cacophony of the birds, but when I strained my ears to hear it I could find it ever-present beneath the irregular riot of birdsong. It was a gentle sound, a background which testified to the continued life of the whole forest, on a timescale of its own, in which the momentary twittering, even the transient lives of the birds, was negligible.

Struck by the contrast between the movement in the forest roof and the stillness of its floor, I seemed to possess once again some kind of intuitive insight into the nature of the forest and its life. It was so much bigger than a man, or a thousand men. Its affairs transcended theirs, ours. Fourteen hundred men and women had come to claim this world, to take it as their own, with the arrogant assumption that the forest could simply be chopped down as and where they pleased, and cleared out of the way. As it had turned out, it had not been possible. Without having the slightest idea why, I was not, in that particular moment, surprised.

The olfactory analysis made by the survey team had analysed everything except the smell of the forest. Perhaps the whole survey report had analyzed everything of the forest but the forest itself. Perhaps the forest as a whole was so much more than the sum of its parts that the whole philosophy of human scientific analysis, taking things apart, descending further and further into a miasma of effects in search of tiny primal causes, was incompetent to deal with the forest.

We even have a phrase for it: *you can't see the wood for the trees.*

The methods of scientific investigation are geared to looking for the trees, never for the forest. Parts, not wholes. Was that why the survey team hadn't been able to find the factor which had doomed the Dendran colony?

I put both my palms flat against the bole of a tree, feeling its warmth and its ancient solidity. It was thousands of years old. Ten minutes with an electric saw could see it felled. How could it strike back? What defense can a tree possibly have against the axe? Evolution doesn't make axes, and certainly not electric saws.

Karen offered me a knife, hilt first.

"Carve your initials?" she suggested.

I gave her a filthy look, and didn't bother with a verbal reply.

She grinned, but with genuine humor rather than mocking irony. She didn't carve her own.

"Which one is the tree of knowledge?" she asked.

I didn't know.

"Maybe they all are," I suggested.

Mariel was sitting apart, with her back to us, looking out across the water at a party of wading birds near the opposite bank. She didn't turn around, and there was nothing to indicate that she might be listening.

"Should I cut some fruit?" asked Karen. "Maybe gather enough for a frugal but Arcadian repast."

"Later," I said. "I'm not hungry."

"You should be."

People are superstitious about eating. They think that if they don't get three meals a day, regular as clockwork, horrible things might happen. Their hair might fall out and their horoscopes might turn on them and rend them limb from limb. Seven years' bad luck. Like all habits, eating gets to transcend necessity.

"Grab what you want," I said, tiredly. "As and when you want. There's plenty around, and you know what's safe. Some of it, anyhow. You can be guinea pig and we'll watch with morbid interest to see if you shrivel and die."

"Thanks," she said. "Can I take the book for reference?" She took the book.

When we set off again Karen was content to lag behind, exploring the vegetation of the river bank with the aid of the book—not by any means an easy task, but one which had to be done and which I was pleased to be able to leave, in some measure, to her.

Thanks to the avenue of clear air above the river we were able to get a better sight of many of the bird species during the afternoon, and I also managed to catch sight of a tribe of monkeys on the far bank. But we found no sign whatsoever that other men had passed that way. There were no marks blazed on the trees, no artifacts abandoned at some point in the past either by accident or design. There seemed no sense in it. I thought of the seven mile wall and the psychological protection it afforded for the people behind it. And yet I could find nothing sinister in the beauty of the forest and its changelessness. It seemed to me to be welcoming, almost *made* for human habitation. There was a magnetic attraction drawing me into its being. How had the people of the settlement resisted it so utterly? And why?

It was not until the sun began to go down that we stopped again, and then both Mariel and I joined forces with Karen in trying to read from the book the most convenient way to gather the substance of a good and healthy meal. Thanks to what Karen had already learned, it was not difficult. The principal problem involved in taking a living from the forest appeared to be the need to climb. There was fruit available in abundance, and there were nuts, but there was more to the gathering of them than simply extending a hand. There were root tubers, too, but they were more difficult to locate, and required digging up and cleaning. Karen wanted me to shoot a bird in order to provide meat, but I refused.

We assembled a rather varied collection of certified-edible material, intending to test out the range of taste-sensations available, to find out what was likeable as well as edible. This was really the most interesting part of the venture, as we had food concentrates in the packs sufficient to last us twenty days, whose only disadvantage was a lack of aesthetic appeal. For the first night, however, we were fairly careful in what we ate, knowing that we were risking stomach-aches as our internal mechanisms protested against the unfamiliar fare. Mariel, in particular, was a little nervous of the fruit. She had eaten the native produce of Floria without complaint or unease, but that had been different. There, even the alien crops were under extensive cultivation. On Dendra, everything remained *wild*.

"How much trust do you think we can put in the advice of the book?" asked Karen. It was obviously an academic question as she had already trusted it enough to fill her stomach.

"As far as it goes," I said. "It's not been put together haphazardly."

"But if the disaster which overtook the colony was unforeseen. . . ." she supplemented.

"They would have added a warning in no uncertain terms," I finished for her. "No, whatever happened to the colony it wasn't anything in this book."

We all accepted that logic.

Despite a relative lack of appetite, Mariel seemed a little more at ease in the evening than she had been when we set out in the morning. She remained quiet, but the walk seemed to have done her good, both in taking her away from the disturbing influence of the colonists and in making her use her body and tiring her out. She seemed relaxed, settled. While Karen and I put up the tent she lay flat on her back on a mound of grass and dozed lightly.

"You know," I said, when I came to clear away the debris of our meal by throwing it into the river, "I can't help thinking that all of this is an existential joke."

"All what?" asked Karen.

"Our dining handsomely on nuts and fruit. The seeds of the forest."

"Why?"

"Because the purpose of seeds is reproduction. Trees grow seeds to make more trees. Or seeds grow trees to make more seeds. Either way the idea is to be fruitful and multiply. But on Dendra, that idea was worked out millions of years ago, just about. The forest is everywhere. There's not only nowhere for it to expand to, there's nowhere for it to *try* and expand to. And trees aren't like people. They don't die so readily. They go on and on and on, getting older and older, with no real need to die at all. They *do* die, for one reason and another, eventually. But only after thousands of years. The forest only needs to be replenished very slowly. And yet, the trees produce seed in abundance, constantly. Not even season by season but *all the time*. It's part of their intrinsic nature—evolutionary priorities which were once vital but are now no longer necessary. An echo of the past. You might almost say that the only reason the trees go on producing fruit is to feed the birds and the insects."

"The same must apply to forests on Earth," said Karen.

I shook my head, but not in contradiction. "In a way," I said, "it happens everywhere. All species tend to overproduce their means of reproduction. But here, where everything is so perfectly balanced, it seems so strange. . . ."

"Sometimes," she said, "you're like a little child." She said it soberly, without any derisory intention.

"Maybe," I said. "But think of it. Trees can go on for thousands of years, just getting older. All the while they manufacture fruit. And yet all that's required, in the long run, is for one seed to replace one tree when it finally succumbs."

"How many sperm have you generated in your lifetime, Alex?" she asked. "Just for your one lone son."

I shrugged.

"Mind you," she said. "You're right about some of it. Some of the stuff is no damned use at all. Tastes awful."

The way she kept on returning to the egocentric viewpoint was faintly annoying. I hoped, perhaps unkindly, that if any one of us were to get sick as a result of a metabolic rebellion it would be Karen.

As it turned out, however, it was Mariel. She woke up from her doze when we lit the lamp, and it occurred to her almost at once that all was not well internally. I gave her something to help settle it, but it was the kind of situation where nothing works wonders. She ached for a long time into the night, and had diarrhoea. Karen kept her company outside the tent while I removed myself diplomatically from the scene. With a small handlantern I set out to explore the night life of the vicinity.

By night, the forest wore a different aspect. The camp was a fragment of alien existence becalmed in an oasis of blue-white light, with an infinite darkness all around. Only from the river bank itself could I actually look up and see the stars. One of Dendra's two moons was in the sky, and though it presented a disc rather than being simply a point of light it seemed no brighter than the most prominent stars.

The sound of the forest abated with the night, but lost nothing in terms of complexity. The birds, save for one or two nocturnal species, were silent, but whistling, whirring, clicking insects took their place. There were bats, too, fluttering about between the trees. Occasionally, I could just catch the lower registers of their constant auditory dialogue with the environment. Though the background noise was much quieter its components seemed more distinct and noticeable. Robbed of sight, human senses next give priority to hearing. But it isn't simply a matter of substituting one set of data for another. We are, by nature, creatures who order our expectations according to experience of a visible world. For us, it is *seeing* that is believing, and "I see" means "I understand". When we are adrift in a dark world, therefore, the sensory environment becomes strange, eerie—often sinister. Fear of the dark is more reasonble than we sometimes assume.

The flashlight I carried seemed impotent as I wandered in the darkness—indeed, it was almost a handmaiden of the bewildering murmurs. It picked out shadows, and partial shapes, revealed just for fleeting seconds the flickering of bat wings, and once now and again would put a gleam into watching eyes. Most of the eyes belonged to tiny tree-frogs, but some did not.

The oceanic rippling of the forest canopy in the unsteady wind sounded, by night, like an ocean indeed, with countless breakers tumbling in the shallows. Against that background the calling of frogs, nightbirds, grasshoppers all seemed rather plaintive.

I wandered around, quite aimlessly, for more than half an hour. I was never out of sight of the bluish glow that emanated from the large lamp lighting the campsite. I dared not go further.

The lamp did not attract insects. I had assumed that it would, but you can't always judge by Earthly standards. Natural selection favors similar forms, often similar behavioral priorities, but there is never an exact tally. On Earth, moths are drawn to flames. On Dendra, they are not. On Dendra, eyes are not so important, and light plays little part in behavioral programming. The moths on Dendra, I guessed, would congregate not about a flame but about an odor.

When I returned to the camp Karen and Mariel were still outside. I knew that it was going to be a long night, but it was only to be expected. I waited until we were all inside and settled before I called Nathan to check in.

I told him how things stood with us, and he gave me a rundown on the day's work at the colony. There was nothing new to report. Everything was continuing. The lack of anything constructive to say weighed heavily on both our minds.

"Alex," he said, trying to voice something of his unease, "you have to be careful."

"I *am* careful," I assured him.

"*Extra* careful. Don't relax. Don't take anything for granted."

"Don't tell me," I replied, somewhat sourly. "You have a premonition."

"If you like," he said. "Call it what you will. There's something badly wrong and I can't find it. I can't even ask the right question. But every time I walk down the hill I feel it's behind me, following me."

"That's old-fashioned talk," I said. "I don't expect it from *you*. You're the diplomat, remember?"

"I'm out of my depth," he answered.

I already knew that.

"What does Conrad think?" I asked.

"Conrad doesn't know what he thinks," Nathan replied. "He's in no better position to jump to conclusions than anyone else. So he isn't jumping. He's healing the sick and waiting . . . or trying to heal and trying to wait. Alex, these people haven't just *forgotten* what their ancestors were about. They act as if their minds are burned out—blown like fuses. Alex, if whatever is here can do that, I'm not even sure I want to know what it is."

That was the darkness speaking. I guessed that it wasn't just Mariel who was disturbed by the remnants of the colony. Nathan was just letting it out a little. He didn't mean what he was saying. I guessed that he was alone, talking to the microphone. Sometimes it's easier to say what you need to say when you aren't face to face.

I knew that the problem was going through and through his mind. He couldn't let it rest. We aren't ever content with ignorance. We always have to know, or at least to attack what we don't know. The only safeguard is faith, and faith was something we couldn't really find here on Dendra.

I wished that I could assure Nathan—and myself—that there was no mind-breaking force lurking hereabouts. But I couldn't. The survey team had survived unscathed, but that no longer figured. Maybe we had a year in hand, maybe ten, but maybe not. Something, somewhere . . .

We just couldn't tell.

"Take it easy," I said. "And slowly. Just keep sifting through the ruins. You'll find something."

"Which ruins?" he asked. "The buildings, or the people?"

It wasn't a happy note on which to sign off.

Chapter 8

Mariel lay in her sleeping bag, but she wasn't asleep. She looked as if she was feeling rough. I wasn't feeling much like sleep myself.

"How do you feel?" I asked her.

"Better," she assured me, not very sincerely.

"You'll be okay," I said.

She nodded.

There was a silence which I felt to be rather awkward. Mainly to break it. I asked: "What do you think? About the whole situation?"

"Wait a minute, Alex," intervened Karen. "This isn't any time for a heavy discussion. Let her sleep."

My eyes went to Karen, then back to the girl. I hesitated, waiting for Mariel to accept or reject the invitation to talk.

"I don't know what I think," she said.

It seemed to be a common complaint. . . .

". . . But something's *wrong*," she added, all in a rush.

It hardly needed saying. But there was a certain anguish in the way she said '*wrong*'. She felt the wrongness much more basically than Nathan or I. It cut straight through to her mind. The people of the colony weren't just people to her. If even Nathan's calm professional approach was shaken, what of hers? She was *always* committed, involved. Her so-called talent, her so-called understanding, that laid her mind open like a gaping wound.

I snatched up my thoughts suddenly, remembering that she was looking at me. It was a habit we had all acquired. Keep an eye out for ideas, try to cut them back. . . .

Even though it couldn't be any good.

64

Even the start, the break in the train, was revealing enough. I watched her, guiltily, and she looked away.

"I'm sorry," I said, feeling rather foolish.

"It's all right," she replied, in a dead tone. It was a formularistic response.

I wished, fervently, that there was some way this wall of doubt could be broken down. Why, I wondered, should it bother me so that Mariel had some knowledge of what want on in my mind? It wasn't as if I had anything to hide. I consider myself an honest man. Why the need to defend, not just the privacy, but the *secrecy* of the world of my mind?

Perhaps, I thought, that's another reason why seeing is believing and the things we hear are both suspect and strange. Because we're so used to telling one another lies —overt, covert, innocent, safe little lies.

I felt that I had to get out of the tent, if only for a few moments. I stepped outside quickly, without pausing to think it over and giving her the chance to use her talent on my hesitation.

I crouched down by the brightly burning lamp. I fiddled with the controls, turning the brilliance down and the heat up. The glow changed color and became ruddy. I spread my palms to receive the radiation.

"You're not cold," said Karen, from behind me. She had followed me out.

"So what?" I said.

"The way you act," she said, "is really tearing that poor kid." She was speaking very softly. She didn't want Mariel to hear.

"I can't help it," I replied. "I suppose you don't mind walking around with your mind naked?"

"I don't resent it the way you do," she countered. "You have to take these things as they come. You've been around talents before."

"Not this one."

"No," she said. "But what is it about this one?"

"I don't know."

"You sure?" She crouched down opposite me, spreading her palms like mine so that there was a ring of fiery hands cutting out the light. But she wasn't cold either.

"She's a fourteen year old child," I said.

"So what makes you uneasy?" she persisted. "Her age, or her sex?"

"That's a bastard thing to say. I have a son two years older than she is."

"And what's he?" she said. "A talisman to ward off the evil spirit?"

I didn't take the trouble to answer that.

"Hell, Alex," she said, after a pause, "I'll say this much for you. As a sympathetic and understanding human being you make a great scarecrow."

"And what gives you the right to sneer?" I demanded, provoked at last.

That one *she* refused to answer.

"I wish I knew," I said, "whose bloody stupid idea it was to send her along."

"She has a talent, Alex," said Karen. "A valuable talent. Maybe it has its drawbacks, but it's genuine. She could be useful out here. Okay, maybe she can't read an alien mind. But she has insight. A special kind of insight—the kind that you and Nathan specifically *don't* have. If we can only help her—if we can only put some trust in her. But you won't. You're *breaking* her, Alex."

"It isn't me," I said. I was thinking of minds being blown like fuses. But Karen wasn't. She was thinking about something else.

"You don't understand," she said. "You don't understand how much Mariel has tied up in this. It's her chance to employ her talent. It's her chance to put herself to some *use*. You ought to be able to figure that. You're a top-class biologist, an expert on evolutionary ecology. On Earth, how much scope did you have for the exercise of *your* particular talent? How much would that talent have meant if you'd never had the chance to come out with the *Daedalus,* to see a whole *host* of alien evolutions, alien ecologies? This is your fulfilment, Alex. And it's hers, too. Even more so.

"On Earth, she was a party trick, a carnival freak. They tried to put her to work, to use her, and they failed. She's a great lie detector, and maybe she can tell whether people are sick in the head . . . but she couldn't ever find a role to play on Earth. You know that. They wouldn't let her. Because they're like you, Alex. Frightened of her. This is her chance to find some *pur-*

pose in her live. Maybe her only chance. Do you think it helps to have you in constant reaction against her? How do you think it *does* feel, Alex? How do you think she feels about you wishing she were back on Earth, out of sight and out of mind?

"You think your job here is solving complicated problems. Spot the hitch, find the answer, Q. E. D., next question please. Your mission in life is to help make these alien worlds safe for people to live in. To you, that's very straightforward. But did it ever occur to you that you might have other responsibilities as well? Responsibilities to the other people aboard *Daedalus*. To Mariel, to Nathan, to Pete? We all have a mission, Alex—in life as well as in our jobs. Do you have to set the kid up as an enemy? Nathan, I may grant you—he can take it. But not the kid."

I had to divert the attack. It was too powerful. I just couldn't sit still and take it.

"You really do have one hell of a soft core under that hard exterior, don't you?" I said. I put as much sarcasm into my voice as I could muster.

It could have made her angry. On another occasion, she might have spit in my eye. But not tonight.

She had one last thing to say, and she said it straight. "She's fourteen years old," she said. "And maybe you don't feel any sexual tension. But *she* does."

I stayed still. She took her hands away from the heat, rubbed them on her pants, and then stood up.

"Don't stay up too late," she said. "We have an early start to make."

Then she went back into the tent.

Chapter 9

I didn't sleep very well. I never do, first night in a strange milieu. The physical discomfort of sleeping on the ground in a crowded tent, together with the mental discomfort of perpetual semiconsciousness, made the remainder of the night unpleasant, and it was a relief to be able to get up with the dawn and prepare to move on. By the end of the second day, I knew, I would have reached a pitch of physical exhaustion which would make it easy to sleep through the second night.

We ate sparingly of ship's rations, not wanting to cause delay or discomfort by risking the inconvenient effects of the alien provender. It didn't take long to get everything packed and to get ourselves back on the march.

The river grew narrower as it began to wander in long, sinuous curves. By noon we had reached a stretch where it ran considerably faster. But as the river headed down the banks became steeper and the rough trail we followed took us upwards, away from the rippled surface. We could see ahead of us a deep gorge whose sides were steep enough to present the occasional bare face of golden-yellow rock, with only patches of tussock-grass and puny twisted trees scattered here and there. There were rocks projecting out of the water, too, and we could see, far ahead, the foam of rapids.

We had a choice. Either we could stick close to the river and hope to get through the gorge near water level, or we could start climbing. It had to be the latter. We had no guarantee of being able to get through at the bottom, and the attempt would be far more hazardous than the slower and steeper way. The climb wasn't something we could look forward to. The warm, humid air was going to make us sweat, and we certainly wouldn't reach the crown of the gorge in one afternoon's walk.

The elevation of the clifftop was much greater than the height of the hill on which the *Daedalus* had landed, and we could at least look forward to a good view when we did ultimately make it. How useful such a view might be we couldn't know. In all likelihood it would show us little more than a limitless ocean of leaves.

The ascent was by no means uniform. There were many ridges and gullies in between our objective and ourselves —far more than our eyes could initially reveal to us. As we walked out the remainder of that day we seemed to come no nearer to the distant target, although we walked aches into our bones, blisters on to our feet, and a creeping tiredness into our every muscle. The miles went by, but they seemed always to be the same miles, over and over again.

The character of the forest changed subtly as we ascended. The trees grew shorter and tended to assume more complex shapes. The higher we went the more starkly obvious these differences became. The boles of the trees were much thicker, and often gave the impression of being woven out of a number of individual strands bizarrely twisted and plaited together. Root ridges radiated out in all directions, breaking the surface because the soil was shallow and unevenly distributed over the surface of the rock. The limiting factor to the growth of the forest hereabouts was obviously the struggle for water.

Higher still, adventitious roots which were flattened into solid walls ran along the contour lines of the slope, forming a complex system of water-traps: gutters and dams to take command of the flow of water during heavy rain. Usually, the barricades were complete, running from tree to tree without a break, showing that many of the trees were not, in fact, separate dendritic organisms, but part of the same multiform being In all probability, many of the tree species typical of the valleys were parts of similar superstructures, united by subterranean roots. How many dendrites might belong to a single genetic and structural entity was open to conjecture. Up here, it seemed that it might be anywhere between two and twelve, but the actual theoretical maximum might have been far greater.

Although there was no question of the entire forest, or even local areas of it, being 'taken over' by a single individual, the degree of co-operative interdependence between different plant species here was undoubtedly far greater than on Earth. These trees had been together a long, long time. They had grown used to one another's company, had adjusted to one another's idiosyncrasy.

If trees have dreams, then this was surely something akin to their Utopia.

Quite apart from the degree of what might be called the social harmony which existed between the individuals making up the forest there was a tendency for by far the majority of the species to be monoecious—which is to say that both male and female reproductive organs were borne on the same plant. Virtually all the flowers were designed for self-fertilization, sometimes insect-aided. Inbreeding was the rule here, not the exception. That made sense. In a highly stable environment the trend must be towards genetic homogeneity, with little heterozygosity in the individual allele-pairs. Inbreeding puts the brake on evolutionary change, preserving stability. Outbreeding, and the wholesale mixing of different genetic complements, is basically an experimental procedure appropriate to meeting the demands of environmental change. It helps preserve the genetic load of recessive lethals and other deleterious mutations. Inbreeding, by constantly pairing up the lethals, weeds the genes out of the population, and maintains the health of the species, so long as environmental constancy can be maintained.

The same assumptions applied to the birds and the butterflies. The striking color-patterns were part of the same system, facilitating mating choice, drawing like to like and helping to preserve and refine genetic consistency. The rich variety of species and the presence of obvious "spectra" of species were testimony to the continual process of incestual refinement. Species subdivided themselves by accumulating idiosyncrasies—a kind of "binary fission" on the evolutionary scale—and the capacity for variation was thus maintained in the vast range of alternative species rather than (as on Earth) by the variations preserved within the gene pools of individual species.

Stability inevitably breeds resistance to change.

That brought me back, as we toiled on up the mountain, to the questions I'd raised earlier about the consequences of invasion. Would the plants taken from the forest flourish under the alien conditions cultivation which the colonists had tried to impose? There had, of course, been tests—but tests carried out back on Earth, under quarantine conditions. The plants of the forest had shown themselves able to put up with a fairly wide range of stable conditions—but what hadn't been tested was their ability to stand up over long periods of time—several generations—to conditions which were *not* stable. On that hillside, where the ships had come down, the colonists, by stripping the land of the trees, had exposed their crops to the wayward whims of *weather*. That was the danger. Not a considerable climatic change, but a switch from a carefully maintained environment, more akin to a laboratory than a farmer's field, to an environment of small but perpetual changes. Was that, I wondered, one of the problems that had plagued the settlers?

Even if it was, I decided, it couldn't be *enough*. There were still the imported crops to grow in the fields, and the indigenous crops could be gathered from the forest. It couldn't have been by any means an insuperable difficulty.

There was, of course, the other side of the coin: the possibility that invasion from outside would upset the delicate balance preserved by the forest what would set off a great ecological chain reaction and destroy the whole system. But that possibility no longer needed to be considered, because if the Dendran colony had proved nothing else it had at least proved the incompetence of that hypothesis. The forest hadn't been destroyed by the invasion. It had proved to be immovable. And the colony had obviously been by no means irresistible.

When we stopped to rest, quite late, our mood reflected our exhaustion.

"The thing is," said Karen, "that it doesn't look a single meter closer now than it did four hours ago." She was looking up towards the still-distant crown of the gorge.

"Further away," said Mariel. She didn't look as if she could carry on. I felt fairly happy—as if I had a good few miles in me yet. But we had to work on the convoy principle—ask no more of the group than the least is capable of giving.

"We're not in any hurry," I said. "We'll jack it in, for today."

Karen looked at the sun speculatively, measuring the hours of daylight left. But she knew the score. "Sure," she said. "No point killing ourselves to get to the top. We aren't climbing it because it's there. We have to go down the other side, and on to God knows where."

I didn't want to spend too much time on the mountain, if only because we were separated from the river, our primary source of water. But it didn't really matter that much. There was plenty of moisture to be found in the forest. We wouldn't go thirsty, even if it didn't rain for a week. Not too thirsty, anyhow.

"Suppose you were leaving the settlement," I mused. "Going elsewhere. As an individual, or as a group. Abandoning what the colony had already achieved and looking for a new start. You might set off following the river. But would you climb the mountain? Or would you pick easier ground and go around?"

They both eyed the crest of the ridge, high up in the clouds, and considered the question.

"Climb it," said Mariel.

Karen nodded agreement. "Every time," she said. "It's damn near due north, toward the sun. They knew that there's a vast plain on the other side, and a lake. If they were leaving their lives behind, they wouldn't make it easy on themselves. They'd go up and over. And on."

I agreed, too. Intuition, or a feeling for human nature, either way I thought that we were right.

"You think some of them *did* leave the settlement and go elsewhere?" asked Karen, turning back to look at me.

I didn't know. But I nodded.

"Why?"

I shrugged slightly. "Because of the forest," I said.

"What's that supposed to mean?"

"It's beautiful," I said, simply. "A damn sight more beautiful than that bare hillside. You'd have to build a wall round a place like that to keep *me* in."

Our eyes met, very briefly. She knew what I meant.

We began to unpack, and to pitch the tent. It didn't

take long, and it left us with a lot of time on our hands —hours of daylight and nothing to do. Mariel was content to lie down and take the strain off her ligaments, but I still had energy in me that wouldn't let me flop like a rag doll no matter how tired my legs were. I wandered off along the slope, toward the edge of the shallow cliff which fell away to the river. I looked over and down. It was a long way, but I didn't find the sight particularly vertiginous. The slope wasn't sheer enough to carry me all the way down even if I did fall. It was safe enough, although there was a good deal of loose stone and soil around.

I found somewhere solid to sit down—a coign of vantage from which I commanded a view of the whole great valley. I scanned the far slope with my eyes, carefully. There was so much of it that my eyes tried to take in too much at once, but I managed to narrow the focus of my attention.

There was a small herd of mammalian creatures grazing among the green patches that formed a mosaic against the yellow rocks of the lower part of the face. They were too far away to see clearly. I had to get up and go back for the binoculars.

"Come and look," I said to Karen.

"What at?"

"Mountain goats."

Another time, she would have laughed, but she had nothing better to do. She came to look at the mountain goats. Surprisingly, after a moment's hesitation, Mariel got up and followed us.

The creatures weren't, in fact, much like goats. They looked more like hairy whippets, no more than a metre from nose to tail. There were about thirty in the herd. It was the first sizable group of flightless warm-blooded animals that we'd seen. The mammals were the least obtrusive of all the forest-dwellers.

"Lords of the world," I commented, when I passed on the glasses. "The pinnacle of evolution."

"What about the monkeys?" asked Karen, who had rather narrow anthropomorphic loyalties.

"Close relatives," I said. "Smallish, dog-like general-purpose bodies. The monkeys are modified for dancing about in the treetops, these for dancing about on the ledges. But they're cousins. 'Monkey' is only a convenience-term—it doesn't imply any kinship, even by analogy, with the human animal. There are no upright mammals with big brains here. If there are any animals with big brains it will be ones that live in the sea. The forest-dwellers are pretty standardized. The predators aren't too different from those things. Even the largest herbivores look like pigs or giant mice. A lot of them still have scales as well as hair, and there's a degree of continuity with the browsing lizards, just as there is between the lizards and the frogs. There's no powerful selection encouraging adaptive radiation, you see. Everything on Dendra is the standard economy model. A slow evolutionary diffusion. Even the birds, apart from their plumage, are physically very standardized. Only the insects, probably with the help of a few million years start, have managed to explore a great many evolutionary avenues."

"I bet the dinosaurs never died out either," she murmured, taking the lecture philosophically.

"No," I said. "They never evolved. . . ."

"Don't bother to explain why," she said, quickly. "I'll guess. It'll be more fun."

I shut up, feeling slightly unappreciated.

Mariel, meanwhile, had tired of the goats and was scanning the distant slopes with the binoculars in the hope of picking up something new. As she swung the lenses round to their limit, looking forward along the course of the river to a green area just visible beyond the gorge, through the narrow crack between the two faces of rock, she stopped.

"Smoke!" she said, in surprise.

I looked where the glasses were pointing. I couldn't see a thing. It was much too far.

"Can't be," I said. "The trees won't burn." But even as I said it I was aware of the catch. The trees didn't burn —unless the outer coating was stripped away and the xylem chopped up to make firewood. . . .

She pointed, handing me the glasses. "It's smoke," she said.

I looked. Even through the glasses the green blur of the land beyond the gorge didn't seem any clearer. I could see the greyish haze which Mariel had identified as smoke, but it was so tenuous. . . .

I altered the focus of the glasses, very slightly, and

realised that the grey haze and the green blur weren't equidistant. The haze was, in fact, rather closer—*in* the gorge, above the surface of the river. It was a swirling cloud, drifting close to a patch of scrub clinging to a crevice above the rushing water. It seemed to sparkle, to change as it swirled. It was a kind of yellow-grey, but it didn't look like woodsmoke to me. And there was definitely no hint of flame. While it isn't always true that there's no smoke without fire, the absence of the latter is at least grounds for suspicion. . . .

The cloud wasn't smoke. It wasn't ascending into the sky, just swirling round and round. It wasn't at the mercy of the wind, which must have been quite tangible in the crack of the gorge. How big it might be I couldn't really tell, because it was too far away, but it must have been quite some size, involving millions of individual particles.

"They're butterflies," I declared. "It's a cloud of insects. The sparkle effect is the fluttering of parti-colored wings. Yellow and white—maybe yellow and blue. There are millions of them."

I gave the glasses back to Mariel, and she fiddled with the focussing device, trying to confirm what I'd said. She didn't like to disbelieve me, but she wasn't convinced. Eventually, though, she decided that I had to be right. It wasn't smoke.

"What are they doing?" she asked.

"Having a party," said Karen, reaching out to take the binoculars to get a look herself.

"Insects often congregate," I said. "It's probably not unusual. We can see that lot because they're over open water. It probably happens all the time, in the forest."

"Like swarms of locusts," added Karen, helpfully.

"No," I said, perhaps too quickly. "That's a seasonal phenomenon."

"Okay," she said, levelly. "Don't bother."

"It looked like smoke," said Mariel, defensively.

I nodded. "No way to tell," I said. "Not at this distance. Not immediately."

"They *are* having a party," said Karen, irrelevantly. "Look at them go."

"We'll get a chance to see it close someday," I said, more to Mariel than to Karen. "It'll be quite something. Perhaps they congregate like that before mating. It may be that there are areas of the forest where such congregations often happen—the geographical equivalent to springtime."

"Yes," she said, without injecting any real meaning into the word. She looked uneasy, still uncertain. For once I didn't have any pangs of guilt about what thoughts she might have picked up in my head that I'd rather have left hidden. I had a clear conscience. I smiled at her. Briefly, she smiled back.

Slowly, we walked back to the camp.

Chapter 10

Nathan called just before nightfall. He sounded tired, and none too happy. The tone of his voice said clearly that there was news, but that almost all of it was bad.

"We cracked it," he said. "The whole thing. Wide open."

"How?" I asked.

"You know that heap of rocks close to the ship?"

"The cairn? At the very top of the hill?"

"That's it. Well, today we finally got round to wondering whether it was only there to mark the hilltop or to commemorate the landing or something else equally useless. We'd gone through every damn building in the settlement and come up with nothing but garbage, and we wondered if maybe they'd erected the monument for a purpose. Pete and I spent most of the day shifting the stones and then we started to dig. It was one hell of a job. Give you three guesses as to what we found?"

"A mass grave?" I suggested. My mind was running along morbid lines.

"A cylinder about five feet deep and a yard in diameter. Made out of twenty millimeter steel plate. Pete had to burn the end off with a torch. And inside it . . ."

". . . was the data bank." I felt entitled to interrupt. I was still owed two guesses.

"The lot. The films, the tapes, and the apparatus. And that wasn't all. We also found the records—the history of the colony, the explanation of what happened."

"Buried under a heap of stones on the hilltop."

"It's a time capsule, Alex," said Nathan. "Preservation for posterity. Preservation for a thousand years, if need be. . . ."

"I get the picture," I said. "Tell me why."

"I've only scanned the stuff so far. I called you as soon as I got the basics worked out. Actually, there's a sort of letter here—addressee unknown. Maybe you could call it a kind of cultural suicide note. It's a bit emotional, but it makes the point clearly enough. You want me to read it?"

"No thanks," I said. "Suicide notes always make me cry. Just tell us what it says."

"The colony broke up, Alex. It disintegrated. Slowly."

"Why?"

"That's the hard part. I'm not entirely certain. I don't think the guy who wrote the note to posterity was entirely certain, either. He spends a lot of time condemning people but not too many words trying to explain or understand them.

"The first generation tried to follow the scheme laid down for them—to clear land, plant crops, gather in food from the forest, build houses, and it began to work, too. For five years, ten, but it didn't continue to work. The Dendran plants they tried to cultivate weren't successful. They grew, but they wouldn't yield. They didn't have a great deal of variety in the stuff they'd imported —it was enough to live on, but it wasn't enough to make living particularly pleasant."

"But they could still get food from the forest," I intervened, trying to hurry him up. "There's one hell of a lot of it. They didn't need to make the Dendran crops grow in fields beside farmhouses."

"That," said Nathan, dispiritedly, "is just the point. They couldn't domesticate the Dendran plants to their own system of cultivation. They couldn't unite the two sources of supply. The farms and the forests remained separate, and the question arose . . ."

". . . As to why they needed the farms at all," I finished for him.

The forest, I'd said, is beautiful. They'd need a wall to keep me out of it. . . .

"It wouldn't have been so bad," said Nathan, "if they'd been able to make a corporate decision. But they weren't. The people who came out from Earth wanted to stay with the ships, with the farms, with what they knew to be safe. They didn't want to take any risks—especially knowing that this world was close to the threshold of acceptable risk anyhow. But the younger people —the ones who came out as babies, or were born on Dendra itself—had different ideas. They were for the forest. If it had even been a clean division of opinion, a polarization of the population into two camps, it might have been okay. The colony might have split into two. But that wasn't the way it happened. There were all kinds of proposals raised, all kinds of argumentative standards. They just couldn't find any measure of agreement, any policy of concerted action. They argued, they fought, and gradually, over fifty or sixty years, the colony disintegrated. They went into the forest, in ones and twos and groups, and the people who were left fought a long, long battle to keep things going, to preserve what they had. A long, long battle which, in the end, they lost.

"The more people went into the forest the harder it became for those that were left behind. And the harder it became the more attractive, by comparison, the forest seemed. And the more attractive the forest seemed, the easier it became to be converted from the conservative camp to the radical, and so on."

"Positive feedback," I sad, dryly.

"And, of course," he went on, "the older generation got older. They died. One by one, the ones who would *never* have surrendered, under any circumstances, died and were put away. And their children . . . what else could they do? They had two choices—to stay with the colony and watch it fail, or to follow the Dendrans who wanted to *become* Dendrans, aliens, abandoning everything they'd brought from Earth."

"There *had* to be a compromise," I said. "A whole series of compromises. They could have kept both, if only they'd tried to work it out. It didn't have to be one extreme or the other."

"They couldn't agree, Alex. They just couldn't agree. And while they argued, they lost the chance. Events overtook them. They didn't have the social cohesion. They didn't have enough to bind them together in spite of their differences. They never really became a *community* in their own right. They were just an assembly, an assembly of individuals which disintegrated under the strains of individualism."

He paused, but I didn't have anything to say. The silence was slightly awkward.

He began again: "I don't know exactly how many were left when they decided to construct the time capsule. Few enough, anyhow, to know that there was no real hope. They did the only thing that was left to them—took the legacy of Earth and made it safe, for the hypothetical day when the descendants of the would-be Arcadians might one day need it again. Then they too went into the forest. They felt they had no choice—the decision had been made for them, by the others. They didn't go to *join* the others—there was too much bitterness for that. They went to make their own way, as one of a score or a hundred separate splinters of the original group.

"And that was it. Those who wanted to, and in the end, those who didn't want to and those who didn't know what they wanted all went to be savages, living the idyllic simple life in the great forest. Every last one."

I was following the string of sentences in my mind, letting them reinforce one another by repetition. It did make a sort of sense. It was crazy, but it was convincing. Much more convincing than the guesses we'd made. We hadn't realized because we hadn't remembered that what people do often seems, in retrospect, to have been quite irrational. We know full well that the patterns in history are patterns formed by the statistical aggregation of vast numbers of individual and idiosyncratic events, actions and decisions, but we insist on pretending that things happened and will happen in an orderly fashion, according to a rational scale of motives. The one thing that history never reminds us of is that motives and explanations are almost always put together *after* the event, not before.

My mind ran on along those rather maudlin philosophical lines until it suddenly struck me that with all his repetitive emphasis Nathan had been trying to tell me something. We might have some answers, but there was still one glaring problem.

"Every last one?" I queried.

"That's right," he said. "That's what the letter to posterity says. We have no reason to doubt it. The plain fact is, Alex, that the people who are in the colony now aren't the relict of the original colony at all, they're the ones who came back, and the descendants of the ones who came back."

"But if that's the case," I said, "if they couldn't make a go of it in the forest, why didn't they dig up the data bank and make a real effort to start over in the settlement?"

It was a good question. But it wasn't really the important question. The important question was a little thornier than that. So far, in the forest, we had seen no sign of human habitation. Maybe that was significant, and maybe not. But if so, the question was: what had happened, here in the forest, to drive those people back to the colony and to make them the way they were now?

It wasn't the kind of question which had to have a dramatic answer. Maybe it was all fairly simple. Perhaps the colonists had fared no better, over fifty years or. so, living the simple life in the forest than they had trying to be subsistence farmers on the cleared land. Maybe the same thing had happened in reverse—disintegration, people going back one by one . . . a younger generation who didn't necessarily know anything about the steel cylinder buried under the cairn. People who'd already reverted, culturally and psychologically, to the savage.

"Alex?" said Nathan.

"I'm still here," I told him.

"Could" they have made a living in the forest?"

"No," I said. "I don't think they could. They were mad to try."

"So what we have here are likely to be the only survivors of the experiment?"

"No way to say for certain," I hedged. "But it's possible. I wouldn't bet either way, at the moment, but if you're hoping that we'll find a thriving community out here, adapting in their own sweet way to the great garden of Dendra, I shouldn't pin too much faith on it."

"You'll keep going, though?" he asked, rhetorically.

"We'll be on our way," I said. "First thing in the morning."

"We'll keep going through the stuff in the cylinder," he said. "If I find anything vital, I'll let you know."

"Thanks," I said. And signed off.

I looked round at Mariel and Karen, who'd been hanging on to every word.

"Well," I said. "We found the corpse and we know whodunit. All we have to find out now is what happened afterwards."

"They must have been out of their tiny minds," said Karen. "Cracking up like that. Abandoning everything to run wild in the woods. They must have been eating something which screwed up their heads."

"I talked to Pietrasante," I said. "Before the lift. When he explained to me why Nathan had been added to the strength. I thought he was just making excuses, but maybe not. He said that the UN was worried—they weren't quite sure how to read Kilner's reports. They thought that the primary reason for the failure of the five colonies might not be ecological problems at all. He said that the colonies might be failing for sociological reasons—because the men of the twenty-second century were not the stuff pioneers ought to be made of. In exporting men of the twenty-second century you also export the social stresses of the twenty-second century. The colonists just couldn't unite into a community, a tribe. They didn't have it in them."

"Come on!" said Karen. "Everybody can get along when needs must. Everyone has it in them."

"When needs must," I said, "maybe so. But suppose people come to believe that needs *don't* must. That's what happened here. They thought they could make it on their own. They thought it was all easy. And so they tried."

On Earth, it's easy to live a completely private life. It's easy to isolate yourself in a crowd. It's easy to be alone even when you're adrift in a limitless sea of faces. The necessities of life come to you through the complex social machinery that's built up all around you, and its processes are quite depersonalized. You don't have to be *involved* with the people who sell you what you need or the people who provide you with the money you need to buy it with. The whole bureaucratic organism functions without high-friction personal contacts. It's easy to live with the illusion—with the reality—that other people are immaterial. They are, in themselves, in their unique personalities. Only *en masse*, as interchangeable cogs within the machinery, are they essential to you and to the sustaining of your private, well-designed existence.

On Earth, every man can be an island. That's been true since the twentieth century.

But the kind of society that makes it easy to live a totally private life isn't the kind of society which can put out successful colonies. In a settlement in a human enclave on an alien world the situation is exactly the opposite. Social machinery doesn't exist. Privacy doesn't exist. The only thing that there is is other people. The cogs can't be interchanged at all. Social relationships can't be reduced to me plus the masses—everyone has to work on a face-to-face basis. People who go out to the stars to start new lives have to make lives that are *new* in every sense of the word.

Colonists have to be willing to try. That's one of the qualifications, not only for going, but for wanting to go.

But being willing to try doesn't make it easy. By no means.

Of course, it *can* be done. People *are* adaptable, psychologically as well as physically. But it always helps you to adapt if there's no choice—if the alternatives are impossible. People adapt best under rigorous conditions. Most colony worlds didn't offer a great deal of encouragement to the man who wants to cut adrift and go his own way. But Dendra was different. It *seemed* hospitable. It offered the illusion of a life of idyllic ease.

The *illusion.*

"You know," I said. "If only the colony had been chosen by the customary balloting, I think they might have made it. People drawn from different social backgrounds on Earth, thrown together haphazardly, are *forced* to try and make something out of their inherent lack of unity. But the Dendran colony was selected on a different basis. A political maneuver. They'd taken it all too much for granted—they were never *prepared*. . . ."

I trailed off into silence. It was a silence which suddenly seemed very profound. And then, breaking into it, came the sound of a cough. The sound came from *outside* the tent.

Chapter 11

Karen began to reach for the rifle. I put my hand on it quickly, held it down. When she looked at me I shook my head. She shrugged, and reached, instead, for one of the packs, to look for one of the flashguns. I waited for her to dig it out, then I turned down the intensity of the light inside the tent. The larger lamp, outside, was not switched on.

I strained my ears, trying to catch the sound of any slight movement outside, but I heard nothing. I moved the flap aside tentatively, and peered out. Though it was not too long since sunset the night, aided by the trees, was already pitch dark. I was tempted to bring the rifle, but I left it, and took the flashlight instead. I eased my body out of the tent to let Karen take up a position by the open flap before switching it on and playing its beam around in a low circle.

The moment I switched it on there was another barking sound, brief and explosive. This time it was less like a human cough. I tried to follow the sound with the beam of the torch but couldn't quite catch up with it. I found a thicket, with the boughs of a tree trailing the top of the bushes, and something moved within. I couldn't see what it was. It had moved back, but it paused. All that the light picked out was the curtain of green.

"Ready with that flashgun," I said, stepping forward. I held the torch out before me, ready to thrust it out to fend off anything that came out of the thicket at me. Experience told me there was nothing to be afraid of, but my heart was racing and I had second thoughts about the rifle.

I stopped, close to the bushes. Nothing moved. The stillness seemed strained and my spare hand began to shake. I rested it against my side, keeping it under control.

"It's in there," whispered Karen. "I can feel it."

It wasn't exactly a comforting remark. She had leapt swiftly to the conclusion that there was an "it" rather than a "he" or "she," but I agreed with the judgment. The second cough had been the noise of a startled animal.

I looked around for a stone to throw into the bushes, but there was nothing near my feet except for a fruit-stone which had probably been abandoned by an animal earlier in the day. It wasn't heavy enough to make much impression on the thicket. I stepped backwards, making my way to the large lamp without turning my back on the hiding creature. I knelt, and carefully activated the fuel cell. The lamp glowed and slowly gained in brilliance until the beam of the flashlight became rather redundant.

Nothing happened.

"It's still in there," said Karen.

"Thanks for reminding me," I replied, dryly. There was still nothing close to hand which I might throw.

"Scream," I said, suddenly.

"Do your own bloody screaming," replied Karen.

It wasn't necessary. Perhaps the light and the conversation were too much, or perhaps it simply got bored. We heard the rustle of the undergrowth as the creature moved away. We didn't catch a glimpse of it.

"Didn't seem to like the look of us," muttered Karen.

"I shouldn't think it'll come back," I said, reassuringly. She moved back to let me back into the tent. "I wouldn't bank on that," she said. "It didn't exactly rush off in a panic. Maybe we should have given it something to remember us by—something to encourage it to stay away."

"I *told* you to scream," I reminded her.

She relaxed, lying back on her sleeping back. She threw the flashgun back on the pack from whence it had come.

"What was it?" asked Mariel.

"A pig," I said. "Maybe a monkey."

"Or a 'This animal is dangerous,' " suggested Karen, referring to the legend in the book printed under the drawing of the cat-like predator.

"Maybe," I said, shrugging my shoulders to show that it wasn't important.

It wasn't until I extended myself along the length of my own sleeping bag that I realized how tired I was. The exhaustion had crept into my body and the moment I relaxed completely I was overtaken by the feeling that I'd not be able to rise again for some time. It seemed to take a great deal of effort just to work my way into the bag.

I think we all slept the so-called sleep of the just.

Morning seemed to descend upon us in no time at all. I was content to doze for half an hour, allowing myself the time for a little extra regeneration of body and spirit. There was no urgency in the way we finally roused ourselves, and it took us longer than it had the previous morning to pack up and make ready to move. But when we finally did set out to tackle the long climb we were physically and mentally prepared. We went at it with some determination, intending to reach the top that day.

It was hard going. I stopped paying any real attention to the surroundings and concentrated on my feet. The pack, which hadn't seemed so heavy during the previous two days, now began to weigh me down, straining my shoulders. The others were equally grim. Mariel's pack was by far the lightest but she carried it as if it was a millstone. We didn't find much to talk about. We took about ten minutes out to rest in every hour, but we generally spent the ten minutes getting our breath back, trying to restore the life to our bodies. This was the time when we were *all* regretting we'd come.

But the target did get nearer. Very slowly. The hard, steady slogging contracted time into one long blur. We weren't constantly looking up, so that every time we *did* look up the ridge was a little closer. That helped us to believe in ourselves. We knew that we'd make it.

The day started out warm and bright, but it clouded over. Within the forest neither the temperature nor the humidity altered at all, but we could see that there was a profound change up above. The clouds were ragged at first, and fast-moving, but heavy grey ones soon moved up and began to mass overhead.

I was sweating so hard that the idea of rain was welcome. It would cool us down. But at the same time I knew that it would also slow us down, and from the point of view of achieving our target I had to hope that it would hold off just long enough. If it started to pour the runnels between the root ridges would fill with water very quickly, and we'd be awash with mud.

We ate on the march, silently and soberly—perhaps even sullenly. I, for one, didn't enjoy it much, hungry though I was.

But in the end, we made it. We got to the saddle of the mountain.

There was maybe an hour to dusk, but the weather was such that we couldn't get much out of the view. From where we sat on the naked rocks near the lip of the gorge we could have seen for many, many miles on a clear day.

But the sky was so heavy that the very air seemed grey. The ocean of green stretched away on either side of the ridge, but soon became lost in a haze of obscurity. There was no possibility of catching a glimpse of the *Daedalus* or the patch of bare earth where it rested, and certainly not a hope of seeing the glitter of water in the large lake which, according to the map, lay a couple of days or more ahead of us.

We sat, too shattered to make camp, and watched the sky gathering over the limitless green sea. It seemed to be the sky, not the forest, which was alive now. The northbound airstream was tangible here, at the exposed crown of the hill, and it cut through out light clothing, cooling the sweat trapped next to our skin by our clothing.

I studied the land which lay ahead of us. There was a long, shallow slope cut in two by the deep slit where the river ran into another valley. The valley was wide, its undulations gentle. Away to the east, on our side of the river, the hills grew into a whole range of mountain peaks. There may have been snow on one or two, but it may simply have been an impression given by the swirling cloud. Away to the west, and to the north, there was a great plain.

The curve of the river was hidden by the trees as soon

as it emerged from the gorge, and in the poor light there was no prospect of picking up its course from the occasional sparkle of light on the water.

"Well," said Karen, watching me while I watched the forest, "there's our haystack. And still no sign that a needle's passed this way in living memory."

"Look on the bright side," I said. "It's downhill most of the way."

She shrugged. "The rainwater's going to be chasing us," she said, dourly.

And, in fact, the rain was already beginning to fall. It came in a rush—a few large droplets and then a torrent. We ran for the shelter of the trees, and then began to wrestle with the tent, cursing our idleness.

There was no way the canopy could keep the water off our necks while we got the tent erected—the boughs simply sagged beneath the assault. The raindrops rattled in the leaves like bullets.

When we were inside and dry it didn't seem too bad. The noise of the rain drumming on the canvas reinforced the sense of security we felt as we relaxed inside. But I knew that circumstances were conspiring to make sure we didn't have it easy tomorrow, downhill or no downhill. As Karen had said, the water would be on its way down with us, making the going sticky and treacherous. We couldn't cope with sprained ankles, so we'd have to be careful, and being careful is always one hell of a bind.

Chapter 12

We had no difficulty keeping dry the next day—we had hoods and gloves fitted to our clothing and the sweat didn't build up inside—but that was just about the only difficulty we didn't have. The only way to avoid the water held and controlled by the forest's ingenious system of root-dam irrigation was to step from ridge to ridge over the puddles, but that played hell with the ligaments in the soles of our feet. The medical kit helped us counteract blistering and prevented any possibility of organic deterioration, but there's no repair for simple strain and the dull pain resulting from it.

We got no further that day on the downhill slope than we had the day before coming up. Our mileage total was miserable, but people can't travel as the crow flies and you have to do what you can on the day. Even on the fourth day, when we were beyond the region of treacherous roots, walking once again on grass and moss which cushioned our footfalls, we weren't in danger of breaking any records. The idea that the settlers had left their houses and their hillside for the simple life in the great green mansions began to seem rather more than slightly stupid.

The weather continued to have its effect on our mood. Karen, whose abrasive temperament meant that she was sometimes not a joy to be with even on her good days, tended to be morose, and the great majority of her remarks—to Mariel as well as to me—seemed to have a definite cutting edge. Mariel, who had hitherto been spared the sharper edges of Karen's tongue, seemed surprised, and slightly distressed. I made the occasional desultory effort to lighten the note of the proceedings, but the endless walking and the dullness of the conditions robbed me of any real enthusiasm. I couldn't find the energy to fight the pall of gloom. Until the vagaries of the weather were disposed once again to let the sun shine none of us felt like doing anything except waiting.

I always felt that the effect that weather has upon us is exaggerated beyond reason. We go through our routine lives closeted by our machines for living in, accustomed to their eternal weatherlessness, so that when we *are* exposed, by a combination of circumstances, we are vulnerable. Primitive man, it is said, used to interpret the behavior of the natural environment in terms of his own emotions: sunshine was equated with pleasure, rain with misery, a storm was seen as anger. We retain such assumptions in the way we think about nature but we have reversed the analogy. We interpret our own emotional inconstancy in terms appropriate to the weather. Pleasure becomes sunshine, misery rain and our anger is an internal storm. We no longer live within our natural environment, but our environment still lives within us.

And in the wilderness, we are at its mercy.

The fifth day, however, dawned clear, and the forest recovered with an alacrity which seemed to me to be almost magical. The rain which had fallen almost steadily for over forty-eight hours was lapped up, absorbed into the soil and the flesh of the forest. The balance of temperature and humidity was recaptured easily. It was amazing how competently the system worked, how efficient was its control. Its self-regulatory powers could only be compared to those of a warm-blooded creature such as a mammal or a bird. It was well beyond the cold-blooded dependence of the insects and the reptiles.

A couple of times during that day we surprised groups of the creatures I thought of as forest pigs. Each time it was a family group without a male parent, but the young were well grown. Karen wanted me to shoot one of the young pigs the first time, and became slightly angry when I declined not only that time, but the second time as well. She accused me, alternately, of hopeless sentimentality and outright cowardice, although the excuse that I actually offered was that it would be inconvenient carrying the meat, and far better, if we felt the need, to wait until we stopped for the night and then go stalking birds.

We had, by now—with a little help from the medical kit—adjusted metabolically to the vegetable produce of the forest, and it seemed quite natural to vary our diet a little more by going on to meat, but I was reluctant to start blazing away with the rifle. The reason I put forward to Karen was, in fact, a perfectly good one, but it was not quite the whole truth. I *didn't* want to start killing the forest-dwellers, because in a way I felt that I had no right. Perhaps it was, as Karen alleged, sentimentality, but I honestly didn't think that it was legitimate for us to take such liberties as a matter of course. I hold, deep down, a conviction that life, if not exactly sacred, at least deserves respect.

That evening, though, I had to carry out my promise. I went out into the quiet, warm evening in search of a large, fat bird. The kind I wanted was a flightless species which scuttled around the forest floor on big scaly feet. They lived on beetles and the occasional lizard, and they were pretty nippy on their feet. But I had the poor bastards at a terrible disadvantage. For one thing, I had the gun, and for another, they hadn't learned to be desperately and specifically afraid of people. They didn't stand around like the ducks in Cokaygne, ready roasted with an EAT ME sign hung around their necks, but they were more than a little indiscreet.

I didn't waste any bullets.

I wondered, as I carried it back to camp, whether the ease with which I'd felled it might be an indication of the fact that there weren't any people around these parts, and hadn't been for quite a while. It was difficult to say. Most of the forest mammals were distinctly shy of us, but that could well be because they were distinctly shy, period. I decided that the evidence was neutral, as neutral as no evidence at all.

Karen accepted with no more than token resistance the decision that as she had had the bird put on the menu it was up to her to prepare it. We still had time before sunset, and Mariel and I saw no reason at all to waste the only spare time of the first thoroughly pleasant day we'd had in what seemed a considerable time. And so we left her to it, and went down to the river bank. We'd not been out of our second skins for some time, except when we'd exchanged them for sleeping bags, and the stale sweat inside was beginning to smell more than we could bear. Our pores needed to breathe for a while, and were in desperate need of a wash. Skin can be infected by its own excreted poisons if it's too closely confined for too long.

The river ran slow and shallow here, and very wide. There were numerous small islands scattered in the middle, and occasional deep, clear pools formed close to the bank by the irregularity of the shoreline. We could see fish flashing silver as they slithered through the shallows, and the air over the water was full of glittering flies and gaudy butterflies. The insects danced in spirals, giving the same effect, on a very small scale, as the 'smoke' we had seen before.

The scents of this region seemed new, and the variety of tree species, now I had the time to look at them, seemed distinctly different. I could still recognize most of them, but one or two were new and the relative frequencies had changed. On the ground, especially near the river bank, there was an abundance of great circular cushions composed of a bushy lichenous species that was also new. Rushes grew in irregular patches where the water was less than a foot deep, especially around the larger midstream islets. There were large thickets of a coarse, stiff-stemmed plant with voluminous yellow inflorescences, which were continually addressed by a particular type of butterfly with black and red patterned wings.

As I stripped naked and eased myself into the water, which was cold enough to send a chill running through my flesh, I couldn't help feeling rather uncomfortable. There was really no need, but it was, in fact, the first time that I had felt myself to be alone with Mariel, naked or otherwise. I couldn't help the sudden renewal of my old anxiety, and remembering at the same time what Karen had said a couple of days earlier. There was no way I could avoid being unduly self-conscious.

I trod water close to the bank and watched her as she entered the water, moving smoothly into a lazy back-stroke swimming action. She was looking up at the sky, deliberately not meeting my eye. Her body seemed very white and very delicate. It did not seem to me to be in any way beautiful, but one cannot deny the consciousness of sexual attraction.

I recalled Karen's words—even if I was aware of no tension, *she* would be. . . .

Deliberately, I picked up the clothes from the cushion of lichen—both sets—and began to rinse them through. The cold had reached into my bones and cancelled itself. I was equilibrating, and the water now felt silky and good. After wringing the water out of the one-piece garments and spreading them out neatly I let myself fall backwards, while the water held me up, received me placidly. I rolled, and allowed the waves stirred up thus to splash my hair and face, wetting my whole body. I swam three or four strokes, and then floated on my back until my arm made contact with a branch drooping low over the surface. I gripped it hard, using it as a fulcrum while I brought my body upright.

There were insects swarming in the air around my head, settling in my moist hair. I ducked under to get rid of them, but they were there and waiting when I came up again. I had to move away from the shelter of the tree.

Mariel was still swimming in idle circles, going nowhere and not caring. She seemed to move very slowly, as though she were a piece of carved white wood drifting in a whirling current. Her eyes were turned toward me, and though they never dwelt on my face for more than a few seconds while her motion carried her round I felt that she was watching me closely—watching me watching her.

"You feel better?" I asked.

"It's cold," she replied. It wasn't. Not really. Just cold enough to be pleasant.

"It's been rough these last few days," I said.

"We managed," she answered.

"Are you glad you came?" It was a stilted question, hollowly artificial.

"With the *Daedalus?*" she asked.

"With us. Out here in the forest . . . instead of staying in the settlement."

"I like the forest," she said. "It's real."

"And the settlement isn't?"

"The people aren't."

I smiled then. The comment, though trivial, seemed appropriate. It was a good, conversational remark. Easy. Not cloaked with too much meaning, or with too little.

She reached out to grasp the same branch I'd released a few moments before, but immediately discovered the same problem. Swatting at the insects with her right arm she drifted out again into the current. She tried to hold herself still in the water, but it couldn't be done, so she moved around me into the shallows, where her feet touched bottom and allowed her to stand shoulder-deep in the sluggish water. When we were both still, she looked calmly into my eyes.

Perhaps for the first time I didn't feel compelled to retreat inside my thoughts, to turn away from her supernatural ability. There was nothing inside my head to be hidden, at that moment. I was quite relaxed.

"You hated it back at the settlement, didn't you?" she said. The choice of phrasing was diplomatic.

I nodded.

"You were angry," she said. "Knotted inside."

"Because I knew that we'd find this colony had failed," I added, not knowing whether it was necessary to explain or not, "and I felt bitter when I turned out to be right. Because if I could predict it, so could others. The colony should never have been sent. It was virtually a sentence of death on the original settlers."

"But you still don't know why," she said. "Do you."

"Not yet," I replied.

She ran her palms back over her head, draining water from her hair.

"You like it here, though," she said. "You're not even afraid."

I shrugged. "I like places like this."

"Away from people."

"Not necessarily."

She didn't insist. "Why is it," she went on, "that you can feel at home here on an alien world when you feel so strange and so dislocated on the ship?"

I lost my balance in the water, and let myself go sideways, toward the bank. I went far enough to be able to sit up in the shallows.

"I don't know," I said. "I've never felt at home inside machines. What I know about is living things. In my mind, I suppose I always live among exotic creatures, alien environments. Those are the things which fascinate me. It's my life—the understanding of natural processes. I don't understand machines. I don't know how a radio works, or a fuel cell, let alone a starship. I don't understand the twisted laws of physics which let us cheat and duck out of spacetime to travel faster than light. I understand all this far, far better even though it's alien."

"And what about other people?" she said, with decisive bluntness.

I was slightly startled, and had to hesitate. "I understand people," I said "as biological entities. Living creatures interacting with their environment. That's the way I see them. But not just as animals, if that's what you . . ."

A butterfly brushed my face and I flipped at it with my hand, blinking.

"Is that why you feel uncomfortable?" she asked. "Because people aren't just animals?" It was a wicked question, but her voice was still level—interested, but not probing. There was a world of difference between the way Mariel asked these questions and the way Karen might have.

"Maybe," I said, prepared to play the game. "The trouble is that people don't tend to see *themselves* as factors in an ecological problem. Delusions of grandeur." I deliberately made light of the issue. But she was serious.

"You're afraid of me," she said—and here her voice quavered slightly as she moved on to dangerous ground—"because you think I can read your mind."

"Can't you?" I countered.

"That's not the point," she said, quickly, refusing to be deflected now.

"I can't help it," I said, knowing that she must know that already. The circularity of the argument would always defeat it. All her attempts to communicate in the ordinary human way had to come to this. How can you talk to anyone, establish a meaningful flow of confidence and information, when you know all the answers and the other person knows that you know? How can communication *not* break down?

A naked body is one thing, I thought, but a naked mind is another. We tried . . . we got started. But where to now? Where next? It was easy enough to see where she wanted to go. She wanted to talk about herself, and about me, and about the effect that her talent had on me. But if, in order to talk at all, we had to silently agree to ignore her talent, how could we even begin?

A quiet minute passed.

Then she took her courage in both hands. "Do you know what I wish for?" she asked. "All the time."

"No," I said, feeling apprehensive about all kinds of possible answers.

"I wish," she said, "that just for a day . . . or an hour . . . or a little while my talent would work the other way round."

Having said it, she turned in the water, lifted her feet, and swam away, leaving me sitting in the shallows. Now, just for once, she was the one embarrassed by revelation.

It made sense.

From our point of view, Mariel had a talent. She had an *advantage* in communication. She could understand more than was said to her. She had an intuitive grasp of languages foreign to her. She could detect lies. She was a witch, a reader of minds—almost.

But from inside *her* head, it had to look different. Very different. In her own eyes, she wasn't gifted but handicapped. In communication, she was at a severe *dis*advantage because she only had words to use as tools. She had no way to get across to other people the kind of complex, multifaceted information she got from them. She could understand, but she couldn't make herself understood.

From her point of view, she was locked inside her own skull—confined, in chains. And other people weren't. Not from her viewpoint. They were *free*. They could make themselves known, honestly, and perhaps completely.

For all her talent, she wasn't very good with words. She couldn't use them as she might. She was nine parts dumb, compared to other people seen through her eyes, heard through her mind.

She was alone. An enclosed entity in a world of open minds. A prisoner in her own introspective confusion.

I remembered, a little painfully, that she was fourteen years old.

Suddenly it was fearfully clear to me why so many talents burn out in adolescence, unable to withstand psychological changes: the growth of self-awareness and self-doubt.

I watched her swim over to the nearest of the mid-stream islets, and pull herself out of the water on to the carpet of moss and grass. She was keeping her back to me, but whether that was because she didn't want to see my face or because she didn't want me to see hers, I couldn't know.

I hesitated for a few moments, and then I followed her.

She was kneeling down on a mat of damp grass, between a clump of plants with wrinkled spatulate leaves and squat purple flowers and a spray of reeds. She'd plucked from somewhere nearby another flower, much smaller, a delicate silver in color. She was twirling it between her fingers. I thought at first she might be crying, but she wasn't. I wondered, briefly, whether she *ever* cried.

I didn't know what to say. I crouched down, slightly behind her, and put my hand on her shoulder.

"She finds it so easy," she said.

"Who?"

"Karen. She doesn't mean what she says. Hardly ever. She says nasty things, stupid things, and still it's easy. You understand her. You like her. Maybe you even love her a little."

"I wouldn't say that," I said, trying to sound gentle but hearing it come out dry and slightly sarcastic anyway.

"But not me," she said. "It doesn't matter whether I mean what I say or not. It doesn't matter whether I say anything at all. You *don't* understand. You can't understand."

"I'm sorry," I said, meaning it. But even in the apology there was a kind of defensive denial. I'm sorry—*but what can I do?* That was the unspoken part.

"You like her," she said again. "In spite of what you say, what you both say. You bitch at one another, and yet you're at ease. You're comfortable."

And what she left unspoken was the agonizing plea: *What am I doing wrong?*

And I couldn't tell her. Because she wasn't doing *anything* wrong. The deck was stacked against her, all the way. The same deck that worked *with* Karen and myself, allowed us to bitch and bind and not mean a word, allowed us to communicate regardless, because we knew one another.

I ransacked my mind for something I could say—something that would help to patch up the whole crazy situation. I wish I could have found something.

I had my mouth open, waiting for words to come and fill it, wishing she'd look at me so that perhaps she could read words inside my head that I *couldn't* find. I wasn't afraid, just then, of having her loose among my inner secrets. She could have had the run of my mind. I really did what to do anything I could to help.

And then there was the sound of a gunshot. Not a flashgun, but the rifle.

And I knew Karen far too well to think that she was firing anaesthetic darts.

Chapter 13

I took a headlong dive back into the water and splashed my way back to the bank with all the haste I could contrive. Mariel followed, but couldn't keep up.

It took more time than I wanted to spare getting into the wet one-piece, but I wasn't going to run naked through the forest into God only knew what kind of situation. I left the seals flapping and grabbed the flashgun that we'd brought with us as a precautionary measure. Then I plunged on into the trees.

There were no more shots, and I wasn't surprised to find when I got there that it was all over. There were no prizes for guessing what had happened.

The bird, plucked and skewered, was sitting over the hot plate which was screwed into the lamp's fuel cell. It was cooking merrily away and spreading its aroma far and wide through the forest. Karen was standing by, with the rifle in her hands, ready for use. She pointed it at me as I arrived on the scene, but rapidly pointed it away again, turning back to stare suspiciously in the opposite direction.

I went to wrench the gun from her hand, but she gripped it still tighter. I looked at the breech adjustment, and found, as I'd expected, that the gun was set to deliver bullets.

"Did you hit it?" I asked, not bothering to suppress the fury in my voice.

"Bastard thing moved," she said. "I would have."

"What was it?"

97

"Cat-thing, Panther, or whatever you've chosen to call it. Sort of brindled brown and black."

"Never mind its pedigree," I said. "Are you sure you didn't hit it? Because if you winged it there's one hell of an angry animal out there."

"And maybe a couple of hundred of its friends," she added. "No, I didn't hit it. Want me to go looking for the bullet to prove it?"

I calmed down. Mariel arrived, looking frightened. Her eyes were bright, and her gaze wouldn't settle, but kept going round and round the tree-caged space.

"It's all right," I said. "It was probably just curious. And there won't be a hundred of its friends. These beasts are solitary. Usually."

I directed another sharp glance at Karen.

"What do you want me to do?" she complained. "It came at me. At the bird, anyhow. I shot at it."

"Sure," I said. "Annie bloody Oakley."

"I don't have the same faith in popguns you have," she said. "And I didn't use a dart because I couldn't for the life of me think what I was going to do with a hundred-weight of sleeping tiger."

"Okay," I said, tiredly. "Okay. But give me the gun, now, hey? And let's get rid of the bird before it attracts more visitors."

"Get rid of it! After all the—"

"Eat it," I hastened to add. "I mean let's eat it."

She handed me the gun, and I changed the ammunition setting deliberately. She scowled. So much, I thought, for being at ease with one another. Perfect understanding. Friendship. A little love. I looked at Mariel; and shrugged. If she could read my mind she could read the thought that it wasn't so damned easy as she seemed to think.

But then I smiled a kind of apology. It wasn't fair. I touched her lightly on the arm—a gesture of reassurance —and I walked back to the river bank to pick up the few odd items we'd left there. By the time I got back things had settled once more into their orderly pattern.

It was getting dark, and as soon as we'd finished what we'd stripped from the bones of the bird, I called Nathan to report our progress.

"At a guess," I said, "we'll make the lake some time

tomorrow. No matter how approximate the map is we can't have that much further to go."

"And there's no sign at all?" he queried, knowing full well there wasn't.

"The forest is its own sweet self," I said. "No hint of disaster, no prospect of discovery. But let's face it, we won't be finding any abandoned tin cans or flint arrowheads. It's a big forest. And if there are people out here they aren't building empires."

"I'm not at all sure it matters," said Nathan, quietly. "Whether you find people or not, this is one world that's going to count against us. There's no way we can turn this into a plus for our side."

I couldn't do anything but make a disgusted sound at that. It was true enough, but he knew damn well what I thought about things.

"This was always a ready-made disaster," I said. "They can't hold it against us."

"It doesn't quite work that way, Alex," he said. "We write the reports, but the documents in the time capsule have a voice of their own, and some of them have some very bitter things to say. They don't talk about survey teams and critical thresholds, or about political maneuvers. They talk about colonies breaking up and about failing to cope. Maybe we know a better brand of truth, but these things are going to sound very powerful in the hands of the other side."

And he was right again. The diary material and the letter to posterity he'd found in the steel canister didn't tell the whole truth—just the truth as seen from the people trapped within it. But that wouldn't figure back on Earth. Those documents would become propaganda in the hands of the neo-Christians and all the other One World movements who wanted to see colonization abandoned for good.

No amount of prettifying the facts was going to make Dendra into an advertisement for man's great future among the stars.

"Suppose you don't find anything around the lake," said Nathan. "How long do you keep going?"

"I don't know," I replied. "Until I'm convinced there's nothing to find. Nothing of anything."

"What do you think are the chances?"

"Of what?"

"Of finding people. And, come to that, of finding anything which will tell us what happened here from the day the capsule was buried."

Honesty, it is said, is the second best policy—behind white lies but ahead of black ones. But I always favored the honest answer myself, when I knew what it was.

"Pretty slim," I said. "When we set out, I was optimistic. But now I'm not. I've got the feel of the forest, and it doesn't tell me a thing. If we get to the lake and find nothing, well, it'll be one chance in a thousand that we can ever happen on the whole truth. We have time, but not much else is on our side. We may have to do the best we can with the remains, and that won't be enough. We can give the people at the settlement a new start, but the one thing we can't give them is any kind of a run. On the facts as we know them they don't stand a cat in hell's chance."

"We need some new facts," said Nathan.

He had what might be called a practical mind. If the facts are against you, you find some new ones.

"Okay, wizard," I said. "*Make* some. Or did you forget to pack your miracle kit?"

It was a bitchy remark. But Nathan took it the way he always took them. Easily.

"Okay, Alex," he said. "Check in tomorrow. And good luck."

"Thanks, Nathan," I said. "Thanks a lot." Insincerity dripped from every syllable.

As the circuit went dead, I glanced at Karen. "Uneasy lies the head," I quoted. "It's a tough job being a committed professional. Sometimes it helps to be more interested in the truth than the illusion."

"You don't sound as if the truth's filling you full of joy," she pointed out.

I admitted it with a perfunctory gesture.

"Why don't you think we'll find people?" asked Mariel. "I know it's a big forest, but they're most likely to be near here. You said so yourself—you said they'd make for the lake."

I nodded. "I thought then that there might have been a large group. I was thinking that the colony may have split in two. But it didn't. It distintegrated. The people went off one by one, or more likely two by two. That changes the odds very much."

"Why?"

"Evolution," I told her. "The parent trap."

But there was no point in being deliberately enigmatic. She might be good at guessing the thoughts that lay behind words but she wasn't about to pluck the whole thing out of my head. "The whole evolutionary sequence of what we're pleased to call the higher vertebrates," I said, "is directional. What the reptiles had over the amphibians was a better egg—an egg with a shell. What the birds had over the reptiles was a shelled egg *plus* a measure of parental care after the eggs hatched. The mammals were the great evolutionary success story because they had the best tricks of all. They had pregnancy and live birth instead of the eggshell and much more parental care. And the human is the mammal supreme because the human species has parental care much more extensive and effective than all the rest. That's the key to survival, you see, that's the kind of fitness which makes us the *fittest*, and gives our genetic complement the highest survival value of all.

"The human infant is born at a much earlier stage in development than most mammalian young, so as to be much more malleable, to have a much greater capacity for survival-enhancing *learning*. This is physical evolution by natural selection, but a *positive* kind of selection rather than the negative kind where the survivor is at a genetic advantage only because his weaker cousins perish on the way. But when this kind of evolution reaches a certain point—a certain degree of parental care and infantile malleability—another kind of evolution becomes possible, and, in fact, inevitable. That's social evolution—the extension of parental care from the biological parents to the whole family group and, ultimately, to the whole social structure. Some kind of social evolution can be seen in most higher mammals, and it's taken to extremes in man.

"When prehistory ended and history began, natural selection was no longer an important force in human evolution. Social forces took over, and modern man—including the men who left Earth more than a hundred years ago for worlds like this one— is almost entirely shaped, mentally, by social rather than biological evolution. Human beings, in any sense that they're recognizable to us, are not fitted by evolution for individual survival or survival in small family groups. If the colonists went into the forest in small groups, every one fancying themselves some kind of Adam and Eve, there's no way they can have survived. No way at all. . . ."

"Unless?" prompted Karen, realising that there was meaning in the hesitation.

"Unless they met up again, gradually came together into a new social unit, learned to live with one another. Some went back to the settlement, and did exactly that, but the experience seems to have cost them dear. For the rest, if they stayed divided, they're all dead. If they joined up, then they'll be gathered at some focal point, some target that might have become a rallying place."

"The lake." This from Mariel.

"The lake," I echoed.

"But you don't believe it?"

"Not any more." I looked the girl square in the eye. "I daren't. If I turn out to be wrong, I want the shock to be a pleasant one."

"I remember," said Karen, "somebody said something once about the sins of the fathers. . . ."

"That's right," I said. "It was their sons. They were in a bitter mood at the time."

"Like you."

"Could well be."

Silence fell. After a while, I looked toward Mariel. She was lying full length on her back, on the ground. She was just beginning to look cold.

I tried to transmit a silent message. It's *not* easy, I was thinking. It never is.

But I didn't see how she could believe me.

I stood up. "We'd better get inside," I said, "in a minute or two. I'll just borrow the handlamp long enough to take *this* down to the river."

This was the carcass of the bird. I stooped to gather up most of the feathers and all of the odd bones we had wrenched off for the sake of convenience. "We don't want anything hungry coming after them while we're asleep," I said. "Might give us bad dreams."

They watched me, without comment, and picked up a couple of oddments I might have missed.

I threw the stuff into the water, and watched the black river carry away the floating debris. I stayed there for a few minutes, leaning on a tree and watching the gleam of the flashlight play upon the ripples. I felt the need to stand still, just for a while, letting time ooze by while I abstracted myself from the complex net of human affairs. It had been a difficult day.

There was a gentle splash, as of some small creature, probably a frog, slipping into the water. It was close at hand, and made the high-pitched background noise of the insects and the occasional whistling of the night birds seem very remote.

I shone the beam of the torch straight up in the air for a moment or two, past the boughs of the tree, as though trying to search out the stars with its tiny eye.

The stars were there, all right, and gleaming. But they glittered with their own light.

I listened, deliberately, for the whispering of the wind, which, everpresent, was so easy to ignore. It was a soft, silken sound, and somehow reassuring.

Then I went back to the tent.

Chapter 14

The next day, we moved on toward the lake.

We came into a strange region where the trees seemed to vary exceptionally greatly in age and health. Instead of the vast majority being giants of incalculable antiquity, with polished bark inviolate, we found a large number in stages of decay, with their solid structure infested by parasites, accompanied by many more younger trees which obviously had not attained anything like the average

age of their companions. This seemed a curious kind of imbalance in such a controlled and homogeneous environment. It was undoubtedly local, but how local we could not tell.

My mind, which had for some days been inclined to use the analogy between ecosystem and individual in thinking about the forest, immediately classified the area as a kind of "wound"—a place of sickness. And yet it was no less full of life than any other part of the forest—perhaps even more so, in that here were the signs of change.

I wondered why. Here, it seemed, the stable forest environment was tainted by a hint of the random. Could regions like this form some kind of reservoir in which the actual *capacity* for change was maintained by the forest? That seemed to be inadequate as an explanation. I considered, instead, the possibility that what had happened here might be some kind of a blight—the result of some interference with the natural processes of the forest at some time in the past.

That seemed more likely. Here, as in the areas outside the boundary wall of the settlement, the forest might be regenerating in the wake of a disaster: a disaster wrought, perhaps, by human hands. But if that were so, I quickly decided, the interference had ended long ago, fifty years and more, at least.

As we pressed on into the area, however, it occurred to me that there might well be another explanation. This cycling of the life of the forest—the death of old trees and the growth of new—might be a localized effect caused by the combination of a thousand lesser cycles. There was, on Dendra, no *season* of rapid change and regeneration. If there was springtime here it was a geographical factor, not a temporal one. It occurred to me that *this*, perhaps, was spring, where insects and animals mated, where eggs were laid and change moved faster than elsewhere.

Once I made up my mind that this might be the likelier explanation I began to see the superabundance of fungi and other strange parasitic growths on the trees not so much as symbols of decay but as symbols of health.

Here, in this part of the forest, things were happening quickly, immediately, and in profusion, whereas elsewhere the tempo of existence was sedate and cautious.

There was no way to know for sure. The others

noticed the change in the aspect of the forest but hardly bothered to comment, let alone ask for explanations. They were both tired of seeing new things, finding ever more kinds of living organism. For them, it was just a chaotic mess of forms and structures. They could not perceive the vital patterns within.

When we stopped to rest in the middle of the day Karen was determined to catch up on the bath which she had missed out on the previous evening. Mariel, possibly feeling that her own swim had been unfairly cut short, supported her in the demand that we spare an hour or so. I bowed to the will of the majority for once, not that I could have denied them if I'd tried. In fact, I wanted to take a look around, to examine more closely the new state of affairs. I left my pack with theirs, at the river bank, and walked away into the forest. Prudently, I picked up the rifle and took it with me.

I felt more relaxed than I had at any time since we had first begun the long walk. I had the feeling of being near to a destination of sorts. I no longer felt the need to go on, to force the pace. And neither, obviously, did Karen and Mariel.

I found a sudden great interest in tiny, intricate detail. I peered closely at flowers. I watched insects as they went about their purposeful daily routines. I watched birds in the crowns of the trees. I looked at the clustered growths on the boles of dying trees, and found—as I'd half-expected—tiny clusters of insect eggs between the cracks in the disintegrating waxen coat. There were millions of them, and there were larvae crawling over the leaves, and pupae clustered in hollow spaces beneath the boughs. It was impossible to say whether the concentration of the forces of insect reproduction were causing the death of the tree, or being permitted by its dying. Both factors worked in complicity. There was no real need for cause and effect.

I sat down, by the bole of a tree, half-hidden by a twist in the gnarled trunk, and was perfectly still. By remaining so for ten minutes or a quarter of an hour I hoped to tempt back some of the creatures which might hide from movement and ostentatious human presence.

I waited, and became slowly entranced in watching a group of small golden birds involved in some strange ritual interaction in the branches of a young tree whose foliage was insufficiently developed to hide them.

In appearance, they seemed absurdly like canaries. But I never heard them sing.

I am not one of those people who lay claim to any extra sense which informs them when they are being watched. For all I know, I might be under near-perpetual surveillance and I would never suspect—never, at least, as long as my other senses were engaged elsewhere.

I watched the birds. They paid no attention to me. If I'd known that somewhere up in the branches a pair of eyes was watching me just as steadfastly as I was watching the birds I probably wouldn't have cared. I have a sense of justice. I was observing the forest and it had a perfect right to observe me.

I probably never would have found out if the observer hadn't become as entranced in watching me as I was in watching the aerial display of the fluttering yellow birds. He could easily have stolen quietly away without ever betraying his presence.

But he didn't. His fascination, apparently, blinded him. He didn't hear or see Mariel coming through the trees, looking for me. Nor did I, for that matter, and she didn't see me even when she was within twenty feet.

Then, in order to aid her search, she yelled, at the top of her voice: "Al-ex!"

I jumped.

And so did he.

Only he was up a tree, and he fell out. He didn't fall far, and he reacted quickly enough to have fallen on his feet. But all I heard was a sudden rattling of leaves away to my right that told me something heavy was close at hand, and a kind of cough: an exclamation of surprise.

It was the cough that really jerked me into action. I had heard the cough before, or something very like it, the night the panther—or whatever—had come into camp. I had the rifle levelled instantly, and as he struggled to loose himself from the bush which had broken his fall, before the sight of him had really registered in my brain —I fired.

The dart took him in the back, under the edge of the shoulder blade. The impact knocked him down, and as he tried to get to his feet again I realized what I had done.

It was only a light dart—meant to knock out some-thing with the body weight of a small dog. He was only a boy—Mariel's age or younger—and he was anything but stoutly built, but the dart wasn't enough to put him to sleep. He made it to his feet. He took a couple of steps, without glancing back. Then he tripped and fell again. The fall must have dizzied him, and the way his heart was pounding after the shock must have dragged the drug around his bloodstream very quickly.

He didn't get up after the second fall.

- We ran over to him, and helped him sit up. His head was bowed, and he was covering his face with his hands. He was shaking his head slowly, almost drunkenly. I took hold of his arm, and was surprised by the lack of flesh on it.

I passed the rifle back to Mariel, and she stood away a pace or two. I let his head droop while I took hold of the dart still embedded in the muscle covering his ribs. I wrenched it out as cleanly as I could. He went rigid with the pain, and his head came up, the hands dropping away.

His eyes were glazed, and his mouth hung open. He stared sightlessly into my face.

I picked him up, cradling him in my arms. He weighed no more than sixty pounds. I carried him three or four paces to the bole of a tree and sat him down there, with the tree supporting his torso. When his head sank for-ward again I grabbed it and tilted it back, shaking it slightly to try and wake him up.

He was high, but he was still conscious.

Mariel was standing back, waiting. She was holding the gun uncertainly. I wondered whether it might be better to carry him back to where we'd dumped our packs, so that I could use the medical kit. While I hesitated I looked him over.

He was naked and dirty. His skin was very pale, not tanned by the sun. The edges of his feet were heavily calloused. There were scars on his body, on his thighs and around the knees in particular. Not only wasn't he in the habit of wearing clothes but he obviously spent a lot of time scrambling around in places where he was likely to get cut. Trees, and thorn bushes. He lived wild. But his teeth seemed quite healthy and his limbs were not distorted by rickets. He was thin, but not suffering from malnutrition.

I slapped him lightly on either side of the chin, trying to help him recover his presence of mind.

"So much for the impossibility of Adam and Eve," I said to Mariel, with heavy self-directed sarcasm. "I wonder whether this is young Cain or young Abel."

Young Cain or young Abel looked me in the eye, and for the first time the dullness of his stare gave way slightly. He *saw* me.

And he didn't like what he saw. An expression came over his face, more than fear—something like horror. He struggled, but I caught hold of his arms. He tried to move back, but the tree wouldn't let him. He cringed, averting his face but flicking his gaze back and forth. I could understand his being frightened but I was at a loss to explain the fact that he seemed to be physically affected by what he saw—almost nauseated. No human being had ever looked at me that way before.

"I'm sorry," I said, feeling very stupid.

I knew the script for this kind of meeting, but I wasn't about to use it. Never in my life had I been trapped in the Me-Alex-Who-You/Take-Me-To-Your-Leader syndrome, and I didn't intend to start now.

I turned round to beckon to Mariel. She was still standing six or seven feet away, but she was watching closely. The moment my eyes met hers she was shaking her head. There was fear in her eyes, too—and *more* than fear.

"No Alex," she said. "I can't. . . ."

I was at a loss. I didn't know what was going on. I was concerned about Mariel. I let go the boy and rose, turning to the girl. But she misinterpreted my action, somehow. She dropped the gun on the ground and put her hands to her face.

"No!" she repeated, vehemently. It was half a scream.

She turned, and she started to run.

But it was too late.

Reinforcements had arrived. And they weren't ours.

There were five of them. And they were coming from the direction that Mariel was trying to run. She would have run right into them. But the moment she became aware of their presence she turned on her heel and ran just as hard the other way—towards me.

For a moment, I didn't know whether she'd run *to* me or right past me. I put out my arms to intercept her and she ran into them. She looped her own arms round my waist and she held on tight enough to force the breath out of me. Her face was buried in my shirt, pressing into my flesh. I knew her eyes were shut. I put a hand on her shoulder, trying to ease her grip a bit. She was shaking. She was literally quaking with fear. Fear and . . .

I glanced briefly at the rifle that lay on the ground a couple of yards away. Then I looked up at the advancing savages.

They *were* savages. They were stark naked. They carried bows and arrows in their hands. Two of them also carried something else—large globular structures that looked like baskets woven out of some kind of plant fibre. They couldn't be baskets because the only way into them were small trapdoors set in the side. I couldn't immediately decide what they were for.

They were all male, three fairly young, two rather older, but by no means ancient. None of them was tall or heavily built but they were wiry. Two of the younger ones were chewing something, their jaws moving steadily to an unconscious rhythm.

They were looking at me from where they had paused ten or twelve feet away. Even at that distance, I could tell that the effect was working. They didn't like the look of me—not in the least.

I was aware that the boy had moved away from the tree trunk behind me. He was making his way to join his fellows, by a slightly roundabout route.

While the situation remained crystallized I tried desperately to work out what was so absurdly wrong.

The boy had watched me, from above and to the side, for some time. Not until he had actually looked into my face—perhaps into my eyes—had the shock set in. And whatever effect I had on him, he had on Mariel.

We didn't need any Me-Alex-Who-You garbage. We had already opened communication. But the messages that were getting across weren't exactly 'Hail fellow well met.'

I felt Mariel's heart beat against my solar plexus. Instinctively, I put my arm protectively around her head.

I had to break the silence.

"It's okay," I said, fixing my attention on the oldest of the group. "It was an accident. The boy's all right. If . . ."

I don't know how I would have continued the sentence. But I didn't have to. The man came forward, his eyes fixed on mine. The fear was gone from his face, now, but the expression on his face was weird. I just couldn't decipher it. It hardly seemed like a human emotion at all, hardly a human face. It was the face of a madman.

I wished that I could go for the gun, but he was already too close. I couldn't make out for a moment or two what he was going to do, but when he threw his bow and the three arrows he carried with it away to the right I knew he wasn't getting ready to shake hands. I thrust Mariel away roughly, trying to get her out of my way. She clung on just long enough and just tight enough to stop me getting into position. Although she got out from between us and away to one side I was taken by the naked man's rush and thrown backwards. I lost my balance and fell, sprawling.

He was on top of me in a second. My instinct said to throw him off, to fight him. But there were five of them, armed, and these, after all, were the people we had come to find.

I relaxed, let him get astride my chest, so that his eyes were looking down into mine. Then I grabbed his wrists, held him. And waited.

I could see every detail of his face. His hair was matted, a tangled mass gathered about his skull. His beard was short, but the hair on his supper lip grew over his mouth. There were particles of food sticking the hairs together. His teeth were sound but stained yellow-brown. His eyes were grey-blue and staring.

He made no sound at all. Not a whisper. But I felt that he was looking into my head. And whatever he found there was, to him, so utterly strange. . . .

His right hand was clenched into a fist, and he was trying to raise it. I knew he was going to hit me with it and I didn't let go. I was considerably stronger than he. In a wrestling match he had no chance. But I don't think he wanted to wrestle. He didn't want to beat me up for firing darts at this young relative. He didn't want to kill me because of an inherent distrust of strangers. There was something else behind the urge to hit me, to hit me in the face.

"No," I said, enunciating the syllable quite clearly. These were the descendants of English-speaking people. Fourth or fifth generation. If they had retained anything at all of their previous cultural identity they *had* to know the word. They had to understand.

But the sound meant nothing. The face staring into mine did not change. The maniac mask was set firm. To this man I was something *alien*—something inexplicable—something he had never met before and about which he knew nothing.

"I'm a man, damn it!" I said. "I'm a man." Again, I put all the emphasis into the word he should have known —*had* to know. But he didn't. There was no reaction. 'Man,' to him, was just a noise.

It was suddenly starkly clear that whatever had happened to these people—whatever event had caught them up entirely, while releasing their erstwhile brethren half-mad to return to the settlement—had been drastic indeed. If the people at the settlement had minds blown like a series of fuses, what of *these* minds?

His hand relaxed and he tried to pull away. This time I let him.

He bounded back and away, toward the spot where he'd dropped his bow and arrows. I sat up and looked at the others—five, now, for the boy had joined them. Two of them had arrows notched to their bowstrings, and they were already bringing up the weapons to aim.

I dived forward, but from a half-sitting, half-crouching position I couldn't get the impetus necessary to carry me far. I was still several feet short of the rifle and I knew as I scrambled on that I wasn't going to be winning any battles even if I reached it.

Then I heard Karen shout, in the stentorian tone that only she could muster: "Cover your eyes!"

I dropped flat, shutting my eyes and drawing up my sleeve to protect them still further.

I heard the report of the flashgun—once, twice, and again. I heard howls of anguish from the white savages. Then I heard: "Okay, you dumb bastard—get the gun and *run!*"

Karen had already reached Mariel and was pulling her to her feet. I grabbed the gun. The blinded savages were in a state of considerable confusion. One had disappeared into the trees, two had fallen and were pawing their faces. Two had moved toward the last sound they had heard— Karen's shout. I tripped one of them and body-checked the other, knocking them both arse over tit. Then, while Karen helped Mariel, I joined the retreat, covering our rear as we ran back toward the banks of the river.

Chapter 15

There was no sign of pursuit. We got back to the packs without any trouble. Then we hesitated, not knowing what to do. I felt dreadfully vulnerable. As if there were no place to hide. The savages knew the forest—they were at home here. If they wanted to hunt us down they could do it. We had the gun, but they had bows and arrows, and all the time in the world.

The first thing to do was to try and get some sense out of Mariel. It wasn't easy. She was in a state of some considerable shock. Whatever she'd read in the faces of those people had been far worse than anything she'd got from the sick ones at the settlement. She knew she had to talk, to try to explain it to us, but she couldn't find the words.

"They're not human," she said, half-whispering.

We let her sit on a tussock of grass by the bank. Karen helped support her body while I held her hands. We were both trying hard to transmit waves of reassurance.

"That's the one thing we can be sure of," I murmured. "Whatever else they are, they're human all right."

"No," said Mariel. "Outside. Not in. The things inside their heads—*they* aren't human."

I looked at Karen. If that meant what it sounded like, it was a very nasty thought indeed.

"Listen, Mariel," I said, gently. "You have to be careful. Think about what you're saying. Are you saying that something else is inside them—a parasite of some kind—which has taken over their bodies?"

She looked up. There were tears in her eyes. "I don't know," she said. "I don't know what happened. But their minds aren't human minds. They're *twisted*. They see, and hear, and feel, and everything—all the senses are *different.* . . ."

"Mariel," I said, as softly as I could. "This is vital. They reacted to you, and to me, just as strongly as you reacted to them. And they didn't seem to recognize even the simplest words. Tell me, do they communicate amongst themselves *your* way? Never mind what that way is, whether we call it telepathy or what the hell—just try and tell me—is that the way they communicate?"

The tears were rolling down her cheeks. She wasn't sobbing. Her body was still now, relaxed and weak. The tears were just leaking steadily from her lachrymal glands.

"They must," was all she managed to say.

It had to be true. It was the only thing that made sense. Loss of language—so quickly—couldn't be the result of a mere regression. These people hadn't simply slipped back into barbarism. Something very profound indeed had turned their minds into something new—something alien. A parasite? Some alien thing which had got into their bodies and changed the entire organization of the mind within the brain? Or had it been a kind of metamorphosis, sparked off, somehow, by something that had happened to them—something they had met *here*, in this special area of the forest?

"Is there anything?" I asked the girl. "Anything at all you can tell us?"

"Not now," said Karen, cutting in quickly. "Maybe later, but leave it now."

I released Mariel's hands. I looked round, now wondering whether there was an archer behind every tree.

"What the hell are we going to *do?*" I said. I spoke the words aloud, though they were directed as much at myself as anyone else.

Nobody answered, least of all me.

I took the radio apparatus out of the big pack, set it up, and began sending a signal to the ship. It seemed to be a long time before anyone answered. Finally, though, Pete Rolving responded.

"Find something?" he said.

"No," I said. "But something's found us. There are people here, all right, but they aren't quite what we expected."

"Need help?"

"Not so desperately that you have to lift the ship. We don't actually know what kind of trouble we're in. We got involved in a fight. We don't know whether they're going to come after us."

"You didn't kill anyone?"

"It's all right," I assured him. "Your beloved regulations are still intact. You can assure Nathan we're sticking to the spirit of the mission. But it isn't easy. There's something grotesquely out of place here. The moment they look at us they practically throw a fit—I think they can look inside our heads much the way Mariel can. Only what they see they don't like. They see something alien, because something's twisted their minds into a pattern no longer human. If they decided to come after us there's no way at all we're going to be able to talk to them. You understand that? *No way at all.*"

"Okay," said Pete. "Take it easy, Alex. I'm not trying to issue orders or hand out advice—here's Nathan now."

"Did you hear all that?" I asked.

"Not all of it," he replied.

I repeated the essential information, in a somewhat less aggressive way. I had had no call to get angry with Pete. Of all times possible, this was definitely the one where I couldn't afford to lose my grip on my self-control.

When I finished the second summary, Nathan said, quietly: "And what are you going to do?"

"I don't know," I said.

"You want to come back?"

Until he asked the question, I hadn't put it to myself. Not in those terms. I did want to go back, but it was the taint of panic that made me want it. I thought it over, trying to be calm.

"We still need to know what happened," I said. "Now more than ever. But now, more than ever, we want to make bloody certain it's not going to happen to us. While we stay here we're under threat both ways. We've got natives playing rough games and we've got some mysterious nemesis lurking round these rotting trees. Look, Nathan, we can't take Mariel any further. She's shaken up badly. We can't risk exposing her to those people again, bows and arrows or no bows and arrows. She has to come back. Karen had better come with her. But I'm staying. I'm going on to wherever these people live, and I'm going to find out one way or another exactly where their humanity went."

"No!" said Mariel, interrupting in the most violent tone I'd ever heard her use.

I stopped, and waited.

She had stopped crying now. She seemed, in fact, to have recovered her composure. It must have required an enormous effort of will.

"I can't go back," she said.

At the other end of the radio link, Nathan was also silent, listening.

"Why not?" asked Karen.

"You *know* why not."

"Come on, Mariel," I said. "No one expects miracles. I'm not prepared to take the risk of exposing you to that again."

"You have to take the risk," she said. "I panicked. I reacted just as they did, blindly, stupidly. For them, that's okay. But not for me. All right, now I've done it once. I've seen it. The second time I'll be ready. I won't panic. I'll get inside their heads and I'll *find out* what's wrong."

"You can't . . ." I began.

"You don't know *what* I can or can't," she retorted, swiftly. "And neither do I. But there's one thing we both know, and that's that *without me the only way you'll ever find out what happened here is by letting it happen to you!*"

Well, maybe that was true and maybe it wasn't. But the force with which she put it across made it seem true, just at that moment. Nevertheless, I wasn't about to accept that logic as a reason for taking her with me.

"Nathan," I said, into the microphone. "She's under your authority. You have to order her back to the ship."

"No," said Nathan.

"In my judgment . . ." I began.

"Never mind your judgment," he said, and to judge by

his tone he was showing considerable restraint in his choice of words. "Mariel can make her own judgments."

"She's a fourteen year old girl!" I objected.

"She's a member of the team," he insisted. "Picked for her talents. She has a job to do."

I wanted to say: You bastard, if anything happens to her. . . .

But I didn't dare. Not with Mariel there. I just couldn't talk over her head like that. Because she wasn't a child. She didn't want to be a child. She was a professional, like the rest of us, because that was the only way she could see to make sense of herself.

Talents grow old quickly.

I lowered the mike, but didn't switch off.

"This is no walk in the countryside," I said, to no one in particular. "We can get killed."

That, however, was stating the obvious. I was way behind the current state of group awareness.

"All right," I said, in a soft and bitter tone. "We play it the crazy way." It didn't seem necessary to add any footnotes about not blaming me for arrows in the back, if and when. Nobody would be blaming anyone.

I said goodbye to Nathan and packed up the equipment again. I picked up the rifle from where it lay, and passed it to Karen. She seemed surprised.

"I thought you didn't trust me with fireworks?" she said.

"If anyone's going to start slaughtering the natives in self defense," I said. "I'd rather it wasn't me. I'm squeamish, remember?"

She gave me a curious look, as if she couldn't make up her mind what I was at. She knew I wasn't simply dodging responsibility.

"Am I supposed to save the last bullet for myself?" she asked.

I didn't deign to reply to that, but simply stood up and shouldered the big pack. I carried a flashgun in my hand. Mariel did the same.

Silently, we moved off, still heading downriver.

Chapter 16

Understandably, we went cautiously and nervously. There was not the slightest overt sign of human habitation, but we knew better now, and we were ready to see people in the shadow of every bush. It was all too easy to imagine a stone-age ambush. But if they were aware of us they continued to avoid us scrupulously. Perhaps they had more sense than we did.

The life of the forest went on quite regardless, but it no longer seemed quite the same. The shafts of sunlight which reached through the canopy to the forest floor now seemed to accentuate the dim shadows accumulated about the trunks rather than to illuminate the dancing of the butterflies. There were still a great many butterflies, and a particular abundance of one species, whose wings were scalloped at the edges, patterned black and yellow, with small "false eyes" on each hind wing. The false eyes were hidden while the insects were at rest, but flashed suddenly as they took off, providing a means of frightening or deflecting the attack of a threatening predator.

The scent of the forest was particularly sweet.

We had been walking for an hour or so when Karen said: "What's that noise?"

I listened. Above the perpetual rustling of the wind there was a new sound—not very different but lower in pitch, harsher. For a moment, thinking only of wind and weather, I suspected thunder, but then I realised what it was.

"Waterfall," I said. "The lake is ahead of us. Not far."

We went forward, sticking close to the river bank. The river flowed into the lake, and if there was a substantial

117

fall then the best place to be would be on the lip of the fall, looking out over the water and the shore.

It was late afternoon, the brightest and most even-tempered time of day. As the river moved toward the cataract it swelled in girth and seemed to run preternaturally still. We began to find spurs of bare rock projecting through the carpet of vegetation, and the character of the vegetation in a band about thirty or forty feet wide along the riverside changed to the more familiar aspect we had encountered on the long slopes. Many of the trees were stunted, and rather more light came through the canopy.

Within half an hour we came to the falls, and were able to look over the shallow ridge at the great lake.

The falls were not deep—perhaps only as high as they were wide, which was something like a hundred feet. Nor were they sheer, for the rock had eroded unevenly, and the water tumbled over a face that was pitted and scarred, interrupted by studs and knuckles of stone which forced the great curtain to erupt here and there into sheets of spray. On either side of the falls was a jumble of naked weathered rocks, containing the cataract like a pair of cupped hands. Beyond these areas there were shallow slopes, like the rim of a dish whose hollow held the placid water of the lake.

The lake seemed perfectly round, although from where we stood we could see only a green blur on the horizon marking its other shore. The arc of the shore which swept away on either side of the falls was neat, almost geometrically perfect. Whether the perfection was an accident of fate, or whether the lake was an ancient crater, the scar of a meteor strike, there was no way of knowing. There did seem to be a kind of ragged ridge dressing the top of the shallow slopes which led down to the water's edge.

The slopes were, of course, no less verdant than any other part of the forest, but the trees were smaller, wider-spaced, and shared their land with a great many more squat bushes, thorn-thickets and canebreaks.

Here it was that the people lived. Among the trees we could see numerous shelters decorated with feathers, their slanting roofs presenting all colors of the rainbow to the sunlight. Many of the dwellings were rounded, looking rather like patchwork igloos with hats.

Our view was limited by the greenery, but we could see

people moving about or involved in particular tasks among the loosely-aggregated shelters. We could see children playing. On the lake there were two long canoes, each manned by half a dozen men, trailing nets in the water. Several more such canoes were drawn up at the water's edge.

We watched from the top of the thumb of rounded stone which sat beside the crest of the fall, partly hidden by a knob of grey rock. We put the packs behind us and crouched so as not to be noticeable. I got out the binoculars and began to search between the treetops, trying to identify the particular work in which the various groups and invididuals were involved.

All the people were naked, but I saw a couple of women working with animal skins, presumably for use in the shelters. I saw other women working with wood—stripping bark with rough stone tools.

There was no fire. Try as I might, I could catch no glimpse of flame or smoke. There was no sound either. The children played, but never called out to one another.

A hundred years ago, I thought, the ancestors of these people were the children of civilized men. Knowledgeable men. And yet they no longer have fire, the primary source of non-biological energy. They no longer have spoken language. They've lost six millennia of history, maybe a million years of evolution. Lost—or abandoned. . . .

But they obviously had what their civilized ancestors had not. The willingness to live together, as a tribe. They were regathered together, united into a community.

I scanned back and forth with the binoculars, looking for something—some little thing which would provide another clue, another piece in the jigsaw. I looked for a long, long time, because I couldn't believe that everything should be as it seemed—quiet, peaceful, serene—a community completely integrated into the ultra-stable everlasting present of the forest.

I had to give up, in the end. My eyes were hurting. I glanced at the others, then after a moment's hesitation, passed the glasses to Mariel.

"A great chance," I commented, "to break the world long-distance mind-reading record."

She put the binoculars to her face, adjusting the focus slightly, without replying. Her face was very serious and firmly set. I looked over her head at Karen.

"It's crazy," I murmured.

"They're alive," she replied. "And they're in a much better way than the shabby collection on the hill."

Telling points, both of them.

"One way or another, though," I observed, "the price of survival here on Dendra seems pretty high."

"It's high anywhere," she replied. "And it keeps getting higher. That's the way it goes."

Just at that moment, I couldn't help feeling that her cynicism was hitting the appropriate note.

Mariel lowered the glasses.

"See anything?" I asked.

"No," she said, tiredly. "I get a faint feeling of unease. Could be something I ate. There's something weird, but I can't begin to fathom it. If only I hadn't cracked up when I had the chance. . . ."

"Take it easy," said Karen.

"Do we go closer?" asked Mariel.

"Not yet," I said. "I want to think this through, first. It's no good charging in there and running our necks into a noose. There must be some way that this whole stupid thing makes sense, and we have to be able to come up with some ideas. Let's for God's sake have some kind of plan of action."

"If it were up to me," mused Karen, "I'd say there's only one sensible thing to do."

We both waited, expectantly.

"Back home," she said, when the pause had had its dramatic effect, "we call it kidnap."

She was probably right. If we were ever going to get close enough to one of these people to figure out exactly what had put his mind through the mangle we were going to have to get him away from the bow-and-arrow-brigade. But the thought of a forced march all the way back to the ship with a tribe of angry savages trailing us wasn't very funny. It could happen, no matter how clever we were in securing our specimen.

"Brute force isn't the only way," said Mariel. "Not necessarily. If I can make contact. . . ."

"It'd take a miracle," I said. "The moment you make eye contact the sparks start flying. Even if you can keep hold of yourself, they aren't going to be so determined."

"So what do you want us to do?" put in Karen. "Sit here and pray for inspiration?"

I couldn't do anything but shrug, annoyed and frustrated.

"On the other hand," said Mariel, who was still doggedly thinking away. "We could combine the two."

There was a moment's pregnant silence.

"If I could just have an hour," she said, carefully, when she saw that we knew what she meant. "If I could just muster everything into one big effort. I could do it. And we could be away before the rest knew that anyone was missing."

"Not necessarily," I said. "If these people are genuinely telepathic—the last rescue party arrived in double quick time, remember."

She shrugged. "We're not going to get anywhere without taking risks."

I looked at her pensively. She was determinedly calm, determinedly logical. She was trying with all her might to put what had happened earlier in the day behind her. She was bitterly ashamed of what she obviously considered her failure. She was forcing herself hard, now. But child or adult, that was a dangerous policy. In this mood, she was a poor risk. Maybe she could do it, but there are some risks which are never worth taking.

"Before we go into another confrontation," I said, in a deadly serious tone, "I think we should do a little more work on the last one. Whatever state you were in, you got into their heads then, for just a few moments. All right, maybe you couldn't make any sense of it then and maybe you can't when you look back from your present state of mind. But you *did* see, just for a moment, whatever it was that frightened the hell out of you. You're feeling brave enough now for a repeat performance, but are you brave enough to go back into your own memory and try and sort it out *inside yourself?* It might be the harder way."

She looked at me hard, then looked away. I didn't press the point.

"Evening's coming on," I said, this time to Karen as well as to the girl. "We aren't going to do anything tonight. I don't think there's much point in moving back upriver to camp, we'll pitch the tent here where there's a reasonable amount of open space. Someone will have to stay on watch all night. We'll use the handlamp inside the tent, no light out here. In the meantime, we watch and we think—all right?"

The sun was sitting atop the water in the west. A thin black line, the shore, formed a bar between the ruddy globe and the sea of yellow fire reflected in the still surface of the lake. The sky overhead was a deep blue. For the moment, the forest seemed almost silent. Even the wind was momentarily quiet.

The instant was crystallized. Time seemed to have frozen in its tracks. I studied the top of Mariel's bowed head, trying to imagine the turmoil within. It was impossible—like trying to figure out what was going on in the heads of these naked savages.

Parasites, I thought. Worms inside brains, gnawing away, filling their grey cocoons with alien consciousness.

It was a strong image. But it wasn't real.

"Hey," said Karen, breaking up the petrified moment. "Trouble—I think they've seen us."

I looked round, quickly, and grabbed the binoculars. Something was going on, for sure. People were looking our way, and one or two were pointing.

When I had the glasses focussed, though, I realized that they weren't looking directly at us. They were looking somewhere to our right, further round the crater's rim. There were trees in our way, but after five or six seconds I was able to catch a glimpse of what was really exciting them.

It was a group of men walking down the slope. Six of them, one no more than a boy, about Mariel's age.

"It's the bunch we met earlier," whispered Karen.

"They should have been back hours ago," I muttered. "Long before us."

"They had business in the forest," she replied. "They weren't just out looking for a fight."

"If they were out hunting," I commented, "they had a bad time." They weren't carrying so much as a bird. They just had their bows and arrows, and the curious spherical things. I focussed the glasses on one of the round things, which was being held very carefully by one of the older men. I couldn't see through the wickerwork, but I knew there had to be something inside it. What?

"It's a *cage!*" I said, suddenly—still whispering, although there was no real need.

"For what?" asked Karen. "Canaries?"

I couldn't see. But I could guess. "Butterflies!" I hissed.

A crowd was gathering around the five men and the boy as they reached the nearest of the rounded huts. The whole tribe was alert by now to the fact that they were back. I glanced at the boats on the lake, and saw the men reeling in their nets, ready to go home.

The sun was dipping into the bar of black shadow that sat atop the fiery water.

The two men carrying the cages went into one of the huts near the center of the group. The children had stopped playing. Men and women alike stopped working. They were gathering, gradually, around that particular hut. They came quickly but unhurriedly, most sitting down, or even lying down, as and when they arrived.

"Looks like a prayer meeting," said Karen.

"More like a union meeting," I replied. I still had the binoculars pressed to my eyes. "Looks like we arrived at the right time. I don't suppose this happens every evening."

"Who knows?" she said.

Minutes drained by. Mariel raised her head to watch along with us. She wasn't happy, but she was interested. We waited.

So did they.

They tended to be grouped in knots of five or six—families, perhaps. They did nothing. They seemed quite patient. They looked at one another, but they didn't fidget much. Like a queue at a supermarket till—quietly philosophical.

The wind seemed to have died, temporarily. Such breeze as there was blew waywardly, as much in our faces as at our backs. I caught faint traces of a weird smell—like nothing I had encountered before. Without the wind to carry it away it hung in the air, drifting and diffusing.

I concentrated on the smell. I concentrated so hard that I didn't notice at first what was happening. I was watching the people. I had got so used to the perennial presence of butterflies and their kin that I hardly saw them any more.

But soon there were so many that I had to see. They were all over: on the slope where the huts were, on the ridge around the crater, in the rocks where we crouched, even over the surface of the lake.

They were gathering—gathering into a flock of incalculable size. And the focal point of their gathering was the village below us. In particular, the hut into which the two cages had been taken. They were the species I'd already picked out as being abundant here. Black and yellow wings, with orange eye flashes. They were everywhere. They didn't seem to arrive in vast hordes, they were just *there*. Everywhere that the eye could see. And the numbers were growing.

Butterflies don't fly fast. They duck, they weave, they drift on the air. They meander along with a seeming total lack of purpose. They didn't seem to be in any hurry now, but they had a purpose all right.

The smell grew stronger, not because it was drifting in the almost-still air but because it was being generated around us now. The butterflies were producing it. And the more there were to produce it, the more arrived in response—positive feedback that would eventually bring every member of the species from miles around, gathered together into one great swirling cloud. Millions— billions of insects, gathering to mate.

This was springtime. . . .

And then I dived for the pack that was six feet away, resting on an apron of rock. I tore open its fastenings brutally, hauling out the medical kit and spilling its contents all over the stones as I ripped it open. I picked up three masks—small gauze filter-masks with self-sealing adhesive edges.

There wasn't time for explanations or apologies. I grabbed Mariel's arm and jerked her up from her crouching position, slapping the mask over her mouth and nose. I ran my thumb rapidly round the seal to make sure it was tight. I thrust one at Karen and trusted her not to make any mistakes while I put my own on. She hesitated for a bare second, then realised the urgency of the matter and clapped the thing on to her face. Her expression told me she didn't know what the danger was, but she had the sense not to wait for explanations.

I knew as soon as I had the mask fitted that I was at least half a minute too late.

My head was already reeling as the air I had taken into my lungs before fitting the mask leaked through into my blood. I exhaled it as fully as possible and dragged new air through the filter. I was safe from further harm, but not from the effects of what I'd already taken in. No more than a few million molecules—perhaps thousands—but enough to take effect.

I was dizzy, and my legs were already beginning to give way. I clapped my hands to my head as the organs of balance in my ears began to go crazy. There were tears in my eyes.

I blinked furiously, and went down on one knee because I could no longer hold myself upright. I couldn't believe what I was seeing. The world was hurling itself at me in a chaotic mass of color and shape. A hammer was driving my eyes deep into my skull and my sense of sight was imploding, sensations crowding in, crushed, intense, and then flowering again deep inside, within me somewhere. . . .

My brain burned as the assault overwhelmed me.

And the butterflies. . . .

They settled on my body, on my face, crawling on my skin.

I fell back, and my head came to rest on bare stone. The feel of the insects was like a thousand needles thrusting into my flesh, the feel of the rock and the pressure of my clothes was an unbearable sheet of fire, a sea of pain. When I waved a hand to stir the butterflies, to make them go away, the very sensation of moving my arm, electrifying the nerves and flexing the muscles, was a sensory overload that seemed to shatter in my brain. It seemed worse than any pain I had ever encountered. But I didn't faint, and I didn't die.

Dragging clouds of flame into my lungs, breathing in and out as deeply as I could, trying to force clean oxygen into my bloodstream, I tried to fight the drug, but its effects were too profound.

It had me, and it wasn't letting go.

And the butterflies clustered on my body, and wouldn't go away.

I still had the presence of mind to wonder if I could take the stuff in through my skin.

I had only a few seconds in hand. I groped for the rifle. It had to be within reach. I knew where Karen had let it rest.

The visual images were still inside me, falling like a cataract through the tunnel that had been my eyes, dazzling my mind.

Somewhere in the prismatic chaos was Karen, and next

to her was Mariel. But how to find them when every slightest touch was like being skinned alive? I found the stock of the gun, like a great cluster of razor blades. I dared not grope at random.

Somehow, I found Mariel with my eyes, and pointed the gun. I fired into the web of bloody redness that had to be her tunic. I couldn't remember, while my brain boiled, what color Karen had been wearing, but as I moved the gun I felt it grabbed, and there was something like a bomb going off in my ears.

Someone was shouting.

She was trying to force the gun away. She thought I'd gone mad. But she wasn't ready for the feel of the barrel, and the river of agony it must have sent up her arm prevented her from deflecting the weapon.

I pressed it toward her—into what I thought must be her body.

Then I fired, and fired again.

The recoil threw me back, squirming over the rock shelf. I was convinced that I was dying. The whole universe was an irresistible deluge of pain and light and sound smashing into my skull.

The gun was between my legs, and one leg was crooked so that the muzzle lay up against the soft flesh of my calf. That accident of fortune was one hell of a lucky break.

I fired twice more.

And then I had to wait.

It all went on.

I didn't see how it could. I didn't understand how my being didn't just disintegrate, spread out like a watersplash all over the rocks, liquefied and foaming.

But it wasn't poison. It wasn't a destroyer. I couldn't even lose consciousness until the anaesthetic darts got to work. The experience, agonizing and utterly horrifying, possessed me and had me at its mercy for seconds which seemed eternal.

It was ripping my mind apart.

The sheer vastness of the internal sensory world opened by the drug was beyond comprehension. I felt myself involved with cosmic forces which flooded through me, forces that I had never known before. I felt utterly and hopelessly vulnerable—and yet godlike, for my inner being was the *core*, the *focus* of this new universe of perception.

It was *in* me, and *of* me.

The pain was unbearable and became meaningless.

The sight seemed to have been burned right out of my optic nerves, and yet I could *see* somehow, somewhere *else*.

The forces wrenching at my mind wanted to twist it, to change it, to make it something *new*—something *else*.

And I spun, like a crazy top, into an abyss where walls of nothing folded about me and accepted me into a deep, infinite hell.

The other drug—the drug in the darts—claimed me for its own, and it was all over.

Chapter 17

It was pitch dark.

The sound of the waterfall filled the air.

I felt as bad as you usually feel coming out from under anaesthetic. No better, but no worse. The effect of the other drug had worn off. I was slightly sick and completely disorientated, but alive and, so far as I was competent to judge, sane.

It took me a few moments to locate my memory and a few minutes more to sort things out into the right order. Then I began to grope around.

The first thing I found was a body. It was fairly large, female and alive. It was also sound asleep. I hauled myself up alongside it, and then had to pause as daggers of pain went into my leg. I reached down, searching with tentative fingers for the little darts embedded in the soft flesh. There were a couple of nasty rents in my clothing, and the wounds where the darts were felt ragged, caked with dry blood. You aren't supposed to fire those things at point blank range. My leg was going to be sore for a long time. I only hoped that I wouldn't be laid up.

My leg began to bleed again as I plucked out the darts, but I was surprised by the ease with which they came out. It was a good sign.

I turned my attention to Karen, then, praying that she had been as lucky. I knew that I'd fired into her body rather than her face, but I could still have done some pretty nasty damage if I'd hit the wrong spot. I passed my fingers rapidly over her prostrate form, and found one dart in her thigh. That was no trouble. When I whipped it out she twitched, but she didn't wake up. Her body weight was a good deal less than mine and the two darts would have had that much more effect. I knew she'd come round in her own good time.

I couldn't find the other dart immediately, and so I began feeling around for the packs. I needed some light.

I found the pack whose contents I'd spilled in extracting the masks from the medical kit, and was fortunate enough to locate the flashlight almost immediately. I flipped it on, shielding my eyes momentarily against the glare. The stab of light recalled, just for an instant, the incredible sensory hell that the swarming butterflies had brought. I shone the beam on Karen's inert body.

The other dart was in her side, between two of the lower ribs. She had fallen partly on top of it. The wound was messy but neither of the ribs was broken. We'd both been lucky. After I'd extracted the dart I directed the light toward the contents of the medical kit, and picked up antibiotics and dressings. I was half way through attending to Karen when it suddenly struck me that something was very wrong.

Something was missing.

Mariel.

I scanned the whole rock shelf with the beam of the torch. There was rock, and dirt, and a handful of dead butterflies. Beyond, there was grass and flowers.

Quickly, I finished dressing Karen's injuries. Then, just as swiftly, I bound up my leg. Then I stood up, and moved slowly around the immediate vicinity. She was definitely gone, and so were the insects.

Carefully, I broke the seal that held the filter-mask to my face. I sniffed cautiously, and then breathed deep in relief. The scent was gone. The wind, reasserting its mastery here at the edge of the forest, had carried it away with the butterflies themselves.

I walked to the water's edge and dipped the soft filter from the inside of the mask into the water. I carried it back to Karen and ran the small piece of damp material across her forehead. Slowly, I stripped off her own mask. She was beginning to stir, but I had to work hard on her to bring her round. While I worked, I tried to weigh up the situation. I had fired only one dart into Mariel. She was so much lighter—somehow, without thinking, I had assumed that one would be enough. But she wasn't *that* light. Forty-five kilos, at a guess. And I was just over seventy. She would have recovered first. She might, then, have left under her own steam.

But why?

She had presumably breathed in as much of the other drug as either of us, and by the same token, it could have affected her that much more. And maybe—just maybe—she had a head start on us anyhow.

Karen sat up, making noises at last.

I supported her, waiting patiently for her to recover. I watched anxiously, not quite certain that she *would* recover. But she seemed okay. My mind was oddly detached. As I contemplated the whole situation it seemed remote, reduced in meaning, like a page in a book or an old picture. I didn't really feel *involved*. My anxiety, my fear, my confusion were all superficial things, like tiny waves on an ocean.

"What the hell happened?" moaned Karen.

"Springtime," I said. "The mating season."

She didn't get it. I wasn't really surprised.

"The butterflies," I said. "In the forest, there isn't any seasonal cycle. The insects don't have internal rhythms to regulate their life cycle. Instead, they spend the greater part of their existence in the innocent business of living, until a build-up happens in a particular place—the kind of place we passed through yesterday. When population density hits a certain level it triggers the release of pheromones, which attract more insects from outside, which builds up the density, which results in the release of more pheromones, and so on. Result—one hell of a crowd. Or perhaps I should say cloud. Millions of the things filling the air with their pungent odor—sex hormones, to attract mates by the million. An olfactory explosion. Instant orgy. The mating dance of the whole damn generation, packed into one small area, one brief moment bang!"

"The savages . . ." she began.

I interrupted. "They triggered it. Deliberately. Those things they carried were cages with butterflies in them. They brought a crowd together . . . to critical mass. They weren't just doing it to promote a forest love affair. They get high on that drug. To them, what we experienced was a pleasant experience—a big kick. Any time they can pick up enough sex-starved butterflies . . . I don't know how often. Once a month, once a week."

"And they *like* it?"

"Oh, it goes deeper than that. Far deeper. That sickly smell, which to the butterflies is just an invitation to the nuptial dance, has one hell of an effect on human metab-olism. It affects the whole balance of nervous stimulus and response. It exaggerated the reactions of the sensory receptors in the brain, and to us it became a massive senstory overload. We hardly caught more than a breath or two. We got the shock effect. But they lapped it up. Because they've *adapted*.

"When Nathan said something about minds being blown like fuses he was dead right. That's what exposure to this drug does. In changing the reactivity of the cortex it changes the whole meaning of patterns of electrical activ-ity in the brain. It doesn't *destroy* tissue, it's not a poison, physiologically speaking. But what it does destroy is the organization of activity within the tissue—it literal-ly rips the mind apart. The effect is temporary, and it's not by any means total, but there's no way that a human mind could survive being put through that at irregular intervals. In order to adapt, you'd have to build a new kind of mind—an alien mind. Or maybe you could run—run like hell to somewhere that you'd never have to face it again. There's the difference between the people at the settlement and the people of the forest. One group were exposed and ran. The rest were exposed and stayed."

"But they couldn't," she said. "Not in a couple of gen-erations."

"They could," I said. "We aren't talking about genetic adaptation. We're talking about something much more subtle, much more malleable—the development of a rational mind within a brain. The kind of mind we have is much more dependent upon the kind of world we experience. Minds can be bent, twisted, changed much more easily, much more quickly, than bodies. The real wonder is not that these people have changed so much but that they have changed so little. They've undergone a metamorphosis—the way they *perceive* their world has been drastically altered, the way they communicate with one another has altered, but they still live a life which is in many ways human, intelligent, creative. The boats, the shelters, even the bows and arrows. . . .

"They're savages," said Karen.

"They're *successful* savages."

She shook her head slowly. She hadn't taken it in—not really. I couldn't blame her. This wasn't the time for expanding consciousness to take in new concepts. I marvelled still at my feeling of detachment, of objectivity. I could see all this, sense it. I knew. I *understood*. I felt almost exhilarated for a moment, the ripple washing away those other superficial sensations, the anxiety, the fear. . . .

Then I remembered. There was a *reason* for the anxiety. Karen had realized too, in the meantime.

"Where's Mariel?" she demanded.

"I don't know," I said, soberly. "I don't have the least idea."

Chapter 18

"We've got to find her," said Karen.

I nodded uncertainly. As a statement of intent it was fine, but in practical terms. . . .

I began signalling the *Daedalus*. Despite the fact that it was about four in the morning, local time, Nathan answered almost immediately. He'd been waiting up.

"All bets are off," I said, wasting no time. "We know what did it. It hit us. Karen and I are unharmed except for minor injuries. Mariel's gone."

"Gone where?" he asked.

"Don't ask stupid questions," I replied, abrasively. "Gone. Of her own accord, I think. If she'd been snatched they'd have taken something else, and maybe we wouldn't have woken up at all."

"Woken up?" he queried.

"We slept through the crisis. I used the anaesthetic darts to put us out. But I didn't use enough on Mariel. She woke up first, and now she's not here."

"What happened?" he demanded.

I told him, fairly succinctly.

"This pheromone thing," he said. "Why did the survey team miss it?"

"Because it's only released at irregular periods, in a highly localized vicinity. You saw the report—thousands of trace compounds of biological origin. Many with nasty side-effects in large enough doses, but never any large doses. You could live on Dendra a year, maybe a decade without hitting upon a build-up like this. But once you're in the right kind of area—and in making for this lake and its environs the colonists delivered themselves right into such an area—you're bound to get caught eventually. We had filter masks and knock-out drops. They didn't. One whiff, and they were in trouble."

"What about after-effects?" he asked. "On you, I mean."

"The drug's biodegradable," I said. "Breaks down pretty quickly in the bloodstream. And the effects are all in the mind. It's not a poison, even though it's rather more than a hallucinogen."

"How much more?"

"About as much as you can imagine," I told him. "All through history people have taken drugs in order to induce weird states of mind, in search of transcendental experience. Well, this is *it*. *Authentic* transcendental experience. Which destroys, and transforms. Miraculous transformation. Caterpillar mind into butterfly mind. Civilized man into savage."

"Or schizophrenic."

"Maybe," I said. "The label doesn't mean a lot, at this level."

"How come any got back at all?" he asked.

"Probably because they only caught a whiff. On the edge, maybe not within a quarter mile of the cloud. We're fairly exposed here—the wind took care of the traces. But in the forest, the air stands still, it doesn't circulate anywhere near as fast. This whole damn region is a trap—a trap they walked into. All of them. It was even baited, I guess. If you saw a million butterflies dancing in the jungle, wouldn't you go take a closer look?"

"And those that got the full dose were changed?"

"Those that didn't die. Don't get the idea that it was easy. Not for any of them. I'd say the experience was probably enough to kill seven or eight out of ten, directly or indirectly. The drug's not a poison, but there are other ways to die. Shock—and having your mind so burned out that you become so much fresh meat waiting for the scavengers."

"It's not a very pretty picture," he said.

I agreed with him.

"Could Mariel. . . ?" he began. He stopped suddenly. He knew as well as I did that there were all kinds of ominous possibilities lurking in the wings. She *could* have taken in enough of the stuff to have her mind blasted one way or another. If she'd breathed too deep—if I hadn't managed to make the seal on the mask secure. And I wasn't sure. There was no way I *could* be sure. I had been working under pretty extreme conditions.

"You've got to find her," said Nathan.

"And where do I start to look?" I answered.

He had no suggestions ready to hand. I glanced at Karen, and shrugged. I broke the connection. I didn't care if Nathan was finished or not. Apparently, he was satisfied. He didn't call back.

"We got it wrong," I said. "The wrong way round."

"What?"

"Finding Mariel. We don't stand a chance. We can try, we can do our damnedest. But in the end, it's she that has to find us. If she can. It's the only chance there is."

She didn't need a guidebook to take her through the implications. There was an awful lot of forest. Mariel had gone without a light. And not only didn't we know *where* she'd gone, we didn't know *why*. We didn't know that the Mariel who'd woken up was the same Mariel that had been put to sleep by the dart. There was no way we could know.

"She may have changed," said Karen, flatly.

I shook my head, but then shrugged.

"Why would she go off," said Karen, "unless it had affected her mind."

I shone the torch on a spot of blood that stained the stone beside my foot. I contemplated the spot absently. The blood was mine.

"I can make a suggestion," I said. "Maybe because she felt pretty much the same as the colonists that left the settlement for the forest, in ones and twos. Maybe because she didn't have enough to keep her here."

I paused. Karen didn't have anything to say. Maybe she was having difficulty thinking the unthinkable. For myself, I wished that I didn't find it quite so easy.

"We feel so superior to the colonists," I said, quietly. "We talk about them, we tried to guess what happened to them, as if they're a kind of crossword puzzle. When we found out what happened back on the bleak hillside we expressed polite surprise, with a little sneer and a little anger, because they were so stupid. They didn't have what it took. They couldn't pull themselves together, live and work as a community. They let their colony disintegrate. How stupid, how weak, how ridiculous. . . .

"But maybe there's another way we ought to look at it. Faced with the same choice—the settlement or the forest —which would *we* have chosen? Suppose that we'd come into the forest and found a carefree population of innocent forest dwellers living happy and pleasant lives? Suppose that the entry fee to the kind of life they *did* find here wasn't quite so high? Suppose there was a guarantee that we could go through the change, that the drug would reshape us, cleanse us, make us free. . . .

"We don't have to choose. We have the *Daedalus*. This is only one stop on our way, a segment of our higher purpose. But they didn't have a way out. They had to make the choice as it lay. Either/or. Either they stuck it out, rebuilding the Earth from which they'd already fled, root by root and brick by brick, in the face of the alien forest, which couldn't and wouldn't co-operate, or they tried a new way, an alien way. They couldn't know *how* alien, but when they set off into the forest in ones and twos they'd *made* their decision, in principle. And in the circumstances, who are we to say that it was dead wrong? Who are we to judge?

"Think about it, Karen—if the *Daedalus* weren't here, if we had to make a life on Dendra, one way or another, what kind of a choice would we have? The settlement, or the lakeside. No compromise, no *deus ex machina*, just what the circumstances allow. And when you've thought that one through, think again. Think about what kind of a choice you might have if the *Daedalus* wasn't so attractive as a way out. Suppose, for the sake of argument, that to you *Earth* was an alien place, a place where you were a freak, without any place in human society. Suppose that in an idyllic corner of a pleasant alien world you found naked savages that were living a life that had, one way or another, something that attracted you. Maybe the savages communicated in the way that you communicate, maybe there was something in them that was curiously close to the thing in you which made you an alien among your own kind. And suppose, just for a moment, that you breathed something in and suddenly you *saw*, you *understood*, how it all might be. . . ."

"You're crazy," she said.

"Sure," I said. "So's Mariel, in her own sweet way."

"That's a bastard thing to say."

I nodded. I didn't much like saying it myself.

"So she's down there?" said Karen. "In the village. Going native?"

"She's in the forest," I said. "Thinking very hard. Alone. Weighing it up. And we've no way of knowing—none at all—how the situation really looks to her."

"I don't believe it."

"A few days ago," I said, "she said something to me. Maybe the only time she ever really *did* say something to me. She said that she wished desperately that her talent, just for a minute, would work the other way, so that just for that moment she could make contact with the world. When she first saw that boy, and the others, she was hit by some kind of horror. But now, maybe, she thinks that there's a way around that horror—a way to become like them, to enter *their* world. And maybe, just maybe, she can."

Dawn was breaking in the east. The birds that sang in the daytime began an uneasy carolling which rapidly grew into a strident chorus.

I stood up and went to the lip of the ledge, to look down at the collection of crude hovels, gathered snugly between the aged trees. The color of the feathers was beginning to show in the faint silvery light. They might be emerging soon, to meet the day, to take up the threads of their lives.

Those lives seemed to me to be utterly pointless. They ate and drank and slept and made love and tripped out in an endless, goal-less closed routine. They found no need for language, no need for fire. But to them, it must all seem different. To them, my life must be pointless and derelict. With the basic pattern of need and life so easily supplied I had nothing in the world to do but make up complex exercises for my mind and body. Such futile, ridiculous things as learning about the universe and taking the human race out into its infinite reaches. Thinking, inventing purposes and motives, imagining crazy cosmic schemes into which it all had to fit, by which it all sought to validate itself. Instead of all that, I could simply be, and dream, and be happy or not, as the case might be. Everything my mind worked so hard on—believing and being, they got in a single orgasmic blast, just by gathering a multitude of amorous insects.

What's absurd? I wondered. When you're standing in the light of an alien sun, what's out of place? Where's the natural order? How do you pretend to fit in?

A couple of women emerged from one of the shelters. They looked ugly. They went about their daily business. I waited, while others appeared, men, women and children, all coming out into the daylight. A boat slid out on to the waters of the lake, yawing and dipping as the paddlers tried to bring it under control.

I watched, half hoping that I might see Mariel, and also half dreading it.

I didn't. She wasn't there. There had been no rational reason for thinking that she would be.

Karen came up behind me.

"Are we just going to stay here?" she asked. "Twiddling our thumbs and hoping for the best?"

I shook my head. "It's only a matter of time before they find out we're here. We can't expect to sit here forever while they ignore us. I don't know what happens if they do spot us, but it would be diplomatic to make sure they don't. We have to be in the place where Mariel would assume we'd be if she wanted to find us—five or six miles back upriver."

"And do we just sit and wait there? Suppose she tries to find us and can't? Suppose she's lost in the forest? Suppose *they* find her before she finds us?"

"Suppose the sun goes nova sometime around midday," I said. Then I hesitated, and finally added: "Okay, let's do what little we can. *You* go upriver and make camp. As soon as it gets dark hang out a beacon. I'll spend the day looking around, I'll go on around the lake a couple of miles, and then I'll cut into the forest. It's looking for a needle in a haystack, but if I stamp around enough I might just get lucky enough to get stabbing pains in my foot. She can't have gone far, and that dart wound won't be comfortable. Pity she hasn't left a trail of bloody drips, or even the dart, to show us which way she went."

She looked at the tears in my trouser leg. "Is your leg up to it?" she asked.

I pointed at her thigh. "Is yours?"

She touched it briefly. "I don't suppose you could have used a hypodermic?" she said. "In the arm or somewhere? Or maybe a pill?"

"I could have made faces at you till you fainted," I said.

She made something of a face herself. I didn't faint.

"You take the tent and the rest of the heavy stuff," I suggested. "I'd better take the rifle. I'm more likely to need it."

She didn't argue. "What about the small pack?"

"No point in sweating ourselves to the bone," I said. "I'll stow it under a bush here and collect it on my way back tonight. Come to that, I'll stow the other pack with it—no point in my carrying that around while I'm not going anyplace."

While she gathered up the camping equipment I began

collecting the debris of the medical kit. When I'd recovered it all I put it into one of the spare packs and looked about for a convenient hiding place. I settled for a thicket that would be easy enough to locate even in the dark. All I kept for my long day's work was the rifle and a flashlight.

When we were both ready, I raised my hand in a mock salute.

"Don't get lost," she said, with a seriousness that suggested subtle insult.

"I won't," I promised, sweetly. "And . . ."

"What?"

"Don't do anything I wouldn't do."

She made another face. It was a better effort. I blew her a kiss, and we went our separate ways.

Chapter 19

I tried, in my mind, to lay out some kind of a grid in order to systematize the pattern of my search. I decided to go round the lake a couple of miles, and then strike out into the forest at an angle estimated to be ninety degrees from the line of the river. After a couple of miles that way I'd turn at a shallow angle and come back towards the lake. Then, zigzagging in a series of acute turns, I'd cover the whole area—maybe four square miles —and end up, if I managed to hold my lines okay, back at the waterfall, late in the afternoon. That way, I'd have a reasonable chance of running across Mariel, if she was, in fact, somewhere within that area.

I wasn't really sure that it was a good idea to split up, but it *was* necessary to make the gesture of searching—

necessary, at least, for my own peace of mind. It seemed important to do everything humanly possible, however futile. Fortunately, there seemed to be as little danger lurking in the forest as there was possibility of locating Mariel. The panthers seemed easily-enough intimidated, and apart from those, we had been threatened by nothing worse than the occasional stinging insect.

My spirits were not exactly high as I began to pace out my predetermined path. Trees kept getting in my way, and my attempts to use the sun in order to navigate as straight a line as possible seemed to place an unduly heavy burden on my concentration. I knew that I wasn't going to be able to conquer the gathering sense of frustration and disappointment that would inevitably haunt the day.

It didn't take long for my leg to begin to ache, and then to hurt. By mid-morning I was cursing my thoughtlessness in leaving the medical kit under the bush; I felt in some need of a local anaesthetic.

For once, I was completely immune to the intellectual and aesthetic attractions of the forest. For the first time, it began to seem not only alien but implicitly *hostile,* no fit place for human beings. Knowing now of one sinister threat it was hard not to suspect more lurking close at hand. There were thousands of species of insect, any one of which, in collecting together into a cloud such as we had already witnessed twice, might build up in the air a physiologically active concentration of any kind of poison. Maybe the black and yellow butterflies were only one item on a long menu of pheromonal thrills available to the new human race of Dendra.

I was unsettled, unhappy, resentful of the whole unpalatable situation.

I trudged back and forth, weaving between the trees, never knowing how far away I was from my ideal grid. I didn't attempt to shout her name, figuring that calling attention to myself was as likely to attract trouble as not. I didn't know whether any of the savages were likely to be drifting about in the forest, or whether they would be aware of my presence if they were, or whether they would care, but there was no point in tempting fate with a series of rousing yells. I was by no means sure that Mariel would respond even if she did hear me. It all depended on why she had gone off in the first place.

I didn't pause for long at any time, although I had to lie down periodically to rest my leg. I kept hunger at bay by plucking fruit and nuts off bushes and trees when I came across the right varieties. There seemed to be a great abundance despite the fact that a sizable tribe, perhaps a hundred or a hundred and fifty strong, lived off the area. Obviously it supplied them easily, as well as the birds and beasts which they hunted.

The day wore on and on.

I found precisely nothing.

I didn't even see any animals of respectable size.

The differences between this region of the forest and those through which we had come had seemed striking on the previous day, but what seemed obvious today were the samenesses. It isn't possible to imagine a forest covering many millions of square miles—human minds just aren't up to that kind of imagining. We can imagine ten, and ten squared, and maybe ten cubed, but we live in a three-dimensional world of perceptions, and after that the number of noughts becomes perceptively meaningless, useful only in abstract calculation. We cannot visualize the difference in scale between a million and billion. We can only calculate, and then admit defeat.

In the mind, everything shrinks conceptually to a magnitude at which it can be handled. We always find ways to make complicated things simple, seeking analogies and theories with which to generalize and categorize. We are rarely aware of the absurdity of our attempts to reduce the scale of actuality to the scale of convenience. But absurd it is to search a few square miles of a forest extending for tens of thousands of miles in all directions, and to know that even that search has been cursory and incomplete. It was in the sameness of the forest that the absurdity began to show itself to me. That same sameness told me what hopeless vanity it had been to expect that I could come to understand the forest on the basis of a few days walk among its trees.

I was assaulted by continual impressions of *déjà vu,* as if the forest were mocking me and my attempt to locate within its vast expanse one tiny lost girl.

And the torn flesh of my leg was giving me hell.

I cursed myself, the forest, Mariel and fate, in rotation. I did it silently, but with feeling.

But I knew, as sometimes you do know, that you just have to go on in a situation like that, and if it's impossible —well, you have to try and *do* the impossible. Because there isn't anything else to do, and no reward in doing nothing.

I had to try. I tried. I failed.

I felt bitter about it—no less bitter because I knew it all in advance. Maybe more so.

When the sun sank to the horizon, setting into the thin grey-green blur that was the far shore of the lake, amid a ghostly haze of grey cloud, I returned to the tower of rock that marked the gate of the waterfall, utterly exhausted.

I lay down, prone, on the apron where we had spent the previous night, sheltered from the view of the savages by the low ridge of rock. Without the binoculars I watched the villagers as they packed up their daily routine and withdrew to their shelters. They seemed completely oblivious, wrapped up entirely in their own lives. I had to quell an insane urge to stand up and howl at them. I watched for half an hour or more, well into twilight, while some small reservoir of strength contrived to reactivate my body, prepare it for the last long march back upriver to Karen's camp.

There was still no sign of Mariel. None whatsoever.

I pulled myself over to the thicket where I'd hidden the packs, crawling not because I was afraid of being seen if I stood, but because it seemed easier. I reached into the open space behind the spreading foliage.

And found nothing.

An arrow of fear struck at my heart. For a moment or two I groped frantically. Then cold reason swamped me, and I began, almost reflexively, to weigh up the situation.

I realized first that I had been something of a fool in thinking that it was sufficient to push the packs out of sight. Sight wasn't so important here in the forest, and the human beings must have adapted their perceptions to that even as the native creatures had. The spilled medical kit must have set up an alien stink that would have carried for miles. Maybe the whole pack reeked. Either way, the savages had been up to investigate something during the day.

I began to add up our depleted resources. All the

camping equipment had gone with Karen. Also the lamps, and the flashguns.

But the radio was gone. We couldn't report in.

It would be no use to the savages. They'd probably smash it up to take pieces of metal from inside it, to make fishhooks and arrowheads. The spare clothing they could probably use. And what else—plastic cups, spare clips of ammunition.

And the medical kit. A dangerous toy, that one. Not something to investigate unwarily.

I tried to remember where the book had been—the guide-book to the forest. That was the one thing that they couldn't need at all, and it was one thing I particularly didn't want to lose. But I couldn't remember. Karen had rearranged the stuff within the packs, and where the book had ended up I just didn't know. But perhaps, if they did have it, it might some day come to mean something to them—a kind of lure, to help them back into the process of thinking, of trying to make *sense* of things.

Could a people without a language ever make sense of written words?

Maybe not, but . . .

I went back to look down the slope at the shelters huddled among the trees. It was too dark now to see anything down there. There was no light, no fire.

I picked up the rifle and pulled the flashlight out from my belt. I began to move away, upriver.

As I moved away from the falls their booming faded and died, and the background of sound was slowly taken over once again by the unsteady rustling of the wind in the treetops. The falls had been monotonous, but the wind was more varied, blowing and ebbing as if beating out some endless rhythmic tune in the eaves of the forest.

The fall of night made the forest—which had already become, so far as I was concerned, a cheerless and oppressive place—into a sinister gathering of shadows. I stayed close to the river, where the break in the cover allowed me the sight of a ribbon of sky, not filled with stars, for the night was hazy with light cloud, but silvery with a faint natural light.

The small flashlight I had did no more than illuminate a circle of ground a few feet in diameter. I played it on the grass ahead of my feet, selecting the easiest path.

The further south I went the darker and quieter it became. The river seemed black and still, discreet and patient in its flow, and there was a *hollowness* to the feel of the descending night. The calling of the frogs seemed duller, more remote. The night-flying moths, picked out occasionally by the beam of my torch, seemed large and slow, ghost-like.

All the events of the past forty-eight hours builts up in my mind to make me far more susceptible than usual to the impressions of the night and the unease such impressions inevitably engender. The imagination always embellishes shadows and shapes with bizarre and irrational form, but the conscious mind usually rejects such fancies immediately. There are times, however, when consciousness, weakened by circumstance, will entertain such notions no matter how grotesque their implications. It is at such times that we say of ourselves that we are haunted.

I was perilously close to such a state.

That night, as it gathered about me, stalked me with the images of a rebel imagination, gave birth to the spirits of all the supernatural fears which never quite die in any one of us.

I heard sounds that were *not* of the forest: sounds much fainter than the wind, much stranger than the eerie calls of the night creatures. Sounds like the rippling of drumskins, deeply buried in the sight-depleted sensory environment, emanating from within myself rather than without. We can, occasionally, become aware of the music of our own bodies: the rhythm of heart and blood, the strain of muscle and tendon. It is not always in silence that such awareness becomes represented in our minds by the impressions of sound. In fact, it is usually into a chaos of sounds that such impressions intrude. They are made loud by fear.

And I was afraid.

In spite of myself, I was prey to fear. I am not a man who walks in awe of nature, and certainly not one who lends the least credence to the power of the supernatural. But fear is a physiological thing that need not be awakened by any stimulus of the waking, thinking mind. There are areas of the personality beneath consciousness, in which fears and anxieties may be stirred.

It was not an open, direct fear that worked in my mind,

but a sly unease that slid around its periphery. It was natural enough, after a bad day and a drug-affected night. But it was none the less discomfiting for being natural.

I found the hand that held the rifle by no means relaxed. It gripped the metal around the trigger-guard with an anxious firmness which suggested readiness for action.

We tend, inevitably, to *translate* such apparently-sourceless fears as arise out of our innate condition. One man thinks of them as expressions of the elemental, empathy with nature or the cosmos, another finds in them the stirring of ancient, primitive things, a pagan knowledge of old gods and existence outside life, a third may think himself in tune with other forces alive and active within the real world, for good or evil, and imagines himself gifted or cursed with extra senses or inherent talents.

Rationality is not always enough to defy such easy translations.

I felt—knowing all the while that it was absurd—that I was the victim of alien forces, beset by something which sought to transform me into an alien within myself, to rob me of the humanity which I fought to secure inside me through the infinite days and nights in which the *real* human world was so very far away. I felt *them*, the naked savages, staring at me from secluded inner eyes, watching me and drawing me out with their new imagination, trying to twist *me* into something incalculable, something weird, something *other* than human.

I am not a trigger-happy man, but I believe that if one of the forest people had appeared before me then I would have shot him down without an instant's pause.

I was hurrying when the darkness became all but absolute. I had already covered a couple of miles and I was convinced (more by hope than by logic) that I might spot the guiding light at any moment. I felt, quite irrationally, that Karen would have stayed closer to the falls than we had suggested in arriving at the distance of five miles as a suitable margin. All this hope meant, however, was that the moments dragged by, stretching out as I passed each tree and found no distant gleam in the darkness.

Natural sounds became distorted in my mind. I was startled by something in the water close by, perhaps a fish jumping or an animal something like an otter turning to dive after taking air. The sound of the splash seemed to be sucked back into the water smoothly and rapidly.

Time extended itself, as it can so easily do. Instead of living the minutes at their steady, natural pace I be-calmed myself within them, lost myself between seconds, disconnected myself from the intrinsic fabric of experience and took myself into some languorous dream-time where-in the fluting of a bird became a long-drawn moan and the soughing of the wind became thin and high—elastic moments, elastic sounds.

I had what is called a *premonition*—an insistent feeling that something dreadful was about to happen.

Sometimes, without the intervention of the supernatural or the long arm of coincidence, such feelings do precede real events. The juxtaposition of feeling born of fear and event born of chance can seal a feedback loop—the event magnifies the fear which magnifies the feeling, which in-vests the event with new fearfulness, and in a sudden crescendo which builds in the leisured space between elas-tic moments . . .

I saw the lamp, pale and lonely, high in a tree, seeming so far away.

And, simultaneously, I heard a curious kind of *cough*.

And as I whipped the beam of the flashlight upwards, tilt-ing my face back to see even while the panic mounted exponentially, the cat-thing leapt, its claws reaching for my unprotected eyes.

Chapter 20

I dropped the light.

As I turned my face away, my cheek was raked by a

fistful of needle points, which slashed through the skin like trails of fire. I brought up the gun, thrusting with it as if it were a shield, but I couldn't shove the beast away. Somehow, it clung, trying to wind its body round the barrel and the butt.

With all my strength I heaved, trying to throw the creature aside so that I could at least fire off a shot. But its weight bore my arms down and my finger twisted inside the trigger-guard, unable to squeeze the trigger. I went down on my knees. The beast seemed to be all over me, its clawed feet still lashing out and tearing where they struck. Most of the cuts were mere scratches, but as I wrestled fiercely for the gun one set of needles sank deep into my right shoulder, tangled with the muscle, and then ripped thighs as it finally fell from the nerveless right hand as though it had been abruptly switched off. I reached out with my left hand, trying to push the predator away. I let go of the rifle with that hand, and felt it fall against my things as if finally fell from the nerveless right hand as well, unfired and useless. I tried to strike at the panther with my own feeble, absurd claws.

I crumpled up, dropping my head as I rolled up into a ball, leaving my arm still free. The needles danced on my back, pulling away strips of my clothing soaked with blood.

I was screaming and screaming, the pent up fear streaming out of me now like a flock of bats pouring out of the hollow of a rotten tree. My mind was whirling, utterly helpless in the furious pace of the event. I couldn't think, I couldn't react.

The gun was gone.

Hand to hand, I fought with the cat thing, trying to catch it with my one good hand and hold it at arm's length. It was not very big, if I could grip it and hold it. . . .

But that was a forlorn and stupid hope. It could tear my arm to pieces. I could feel its hot breath, very close, and I could see in my inner eye the jaws gaping wide, groping to enfold my flesh, to crack my bones. I couldn't see with any but my inner eye—I couldn't even see the eyes—the eyes that would surely glow with the wierd, fugitive light that seems to invest cat's eyes even in the darkest night.

It couldn't reach me with the teeth. I was bigger, stronger, with a better reach. The beast had the advan-

tage of speed, surprise, a better natural armory and a lifetime of practice, but even at the level of tooth-and-claw
a man can fight. I rolled sideways, and shot out a booted
foot, which caught the creature somewhere in the body
and brought a satisfying yelp of pain. It also stopped the
claws raking at my good arm. I lashed out again, and
missed, but the creature had retreated a little. It came
forward again, but I intercepted it with the foot, locating
it by sound and feel, reacting by sheer instinct. I kept it
back, away from my soft belly, my throat, my groin.

Without any thought of how the battle might end I
fought on, driven by panic.

I had the strength, but not the skill. I didn't have whatever it takes to wrestle a panther and strangle it or snap
its neck. If my reflexes were following any inbuilt strategy
at all, they were trying to do to the beast what I had
feared in that first nightmare moment that it might do to
me: rip out the eyes, tear away the precious, if presently
useless, sense of sight.

I was lost somewhere in the pain, just as I had been
when the butterfly pheromone had exploded in my mind.
The hurting was already meaningless, spread throughout
my body.

My screams were out of breath.

Then an unbearable light burst in my face. Sound exploded in my ears. I was deaf and blind.

The sound was repeated, twice more. My eyes had
closed tight, but I could not have seen the light. In
deference to the shock, I curled up tight again, hiding myself in a cocoon of arms and legs.

The cutting claws were gone.

I felt something being dragged from beneath my body
—the rifle. I waited. I knew that someone knelt close to
me, and I felt the glow of a flashlight on my cheek.

I heard her speak, and her voice sounded very faint,
blurred, as though it came from a great distance. I missed
the words, but I knew it was an exclamation of horror—
an anguished whisper.

I knew that the light was shining on a mask of ribboned
flesh, colored with blood.

Unseeing, I reached out for her. My fingertips, the left
hand, found the flesh of her arm, but she flinched away. I
knew why. My fingers were wet with blood. My blood.

There was nothing I could find to say better or more convincing than: "I'm all right. I'm all right." Quite ridiculous. But I *was* all right, inside, where it counts. The surface was ploughed up, and I'd lost the feel of my right arm, but I was all right. With one exception the cuts were skin deep. I might not be beautiful but I wasn't dead, not by a long way.

I was hardly conscious of the pain. Or the shock. All that seemed past. I felt, in fact, strangely calm, and my mind was clearing even though my senses lagged.

"Get the medikit," I said, slurring the words very slightly.

"I haven't got it," she said. "You have."

I remembered. No dressings. No plastic spray to stop the bleeding, cover the torn flesh. No patches and thread. Only anaesthetic. We still had anaesthetic. A whole cartridge clip full.

I almost felt like laughing.

"Help me up," I murmured.

I was still blind from the flash, but there was no permanent damage there. My senses would recover. My arm I could do without for a few days. Conrad, with the aid of the *Daedalus*'s technical resources, could have put Humpty Dumpty back together again without the yolk spoiling. The one important question was whether I could walk. I'd lost a lot of blood. People in worse states had walked long distances in times past, but a lot of people had died, too. Karen helped me to my feet, getting herself all bloody in the process. I could stand. But I didn't feel safe. I felt perilously weak.

"Where is it?" she asked, speaking with exaggerated clarity, in case I couldn't hear. "The medical stuff?"

"Gone," I whispered. "The savages. The kit and the radio. And it's . . . a bloody long way home."

"On my God," she said. I felt her arms gently pressing me back down again. I sat. I felt the light playing on my face again. I felt its warmth first and then, by degrees, its glow began to filter through my shocked optic nerves, making my brain frame blurred images again.

I couldn't see Karen yet, though.

"My shoulder's bad," I said. "I can't use the arm. But nothing else is likely to cripple me. Look me over. If you find arterial blood I'm in trouble. If not . . ."

I didn't know what, if not.

She began to look closely at my wounds. I began, then, to feel the pain again. Not that it had ever gone away, but it had become an unsteady background, like the sound of the wind in the trees. Now it began to be perceptible again in all its myriad elements. I could even feel the ripped shoulder. I glanced down at that—the worst of my injuries—and was surprised to find it so presentable. I decided that the nerve, in all probability, hadn't been cut, but merely shocked.

But there was blood everywhere. Too much blood.

"I'm sorry," I whispered, to Karen.

"For what?" she asked.

"I didn't find her."

She didn't say anything to that.

"They stole everything," I said, changing the subject. "We can't call for help."

She hesitated for a moment, and then said: "We're going to need help, Alex. You'll never make it back to the ship. Not on foot."

I was silent. I weighed up what she was saying. My mind was veering crazily. I was okay. I could walk for days. I was hurt badly. I couldn't walk a mile.

I didn't know. There was just no way I could guess from the way I felt. I felt so strange, so completely different from anything I'd felt before. I looked again at my shoulder, still feeling the same sense of idiotic objectivity.

"I'm not going to die," I said, with naive conviction.

"No," she said. "You're not going to die. Not tonight, not tomorrow, not in a week or a fortnight. But you're a big boy, Alex. I can't carry you. Not up and down that mountain. You've lost a lot of blood and a lot of skin. We can't dress the wounds and we can't stop infection. The pain is going to have you in knots."

"Thanks," I said, dully.

"Oh, hell, Alex, what am I supposed to say?" There was anguish in her voice. She felt that she was doing it all wrong. She hadn't much of a bedside manner.

"It's okay," I said. "We stay here. For a while. I'll get better. I'll heal. There's not so much danger of infection. Do we still have the book?"

"The book?"

"The guide-book. I couldn't remember, do you have it or do they?"

"I have it," she said. "It's back at the tent."

"That's one to us," I said. "How to survive in the forest. It has notes on the medicinal qualities of local plants. We can cope, Karen. I'll get better. And besides—"

"Well?"

"We have to wait for Mariel," I whispered.

The world was sliding into focus again. In my eyes, in my mind. I couldn't see Karen's face. It was in the darkness, behind the glow of the flashlight. But I knew she was looking at me.

"You might lose the use of that arm," she said.

Another thought, similarly dreadful, had just struck me. "And my face," I said. "If these slashes heal, without help, I'll be scarred for life."

She didn't answer.

"Lucky I wasn't handsome to start with," I murmured.

Curiously, the thought of a scarred face seemed worse to me at that moment than the prospect of a crippled arm. I don't know why. Maybe vanity, but a face means a great deal. A face is an identity. We recognize people in their faces. Seeing is believing. If it came to a choice between a face and a good right arm. . . .

But there wasn't any choice. None at all.

"We have to get to the tent," said Karen. "I'll help you."

"How far?" I asked.

"Fifty paces," she answered, and added. "But we'll take smaller steps."

"I'll crawl," I told her. I meant: if need be. I didn't have to say that.

She helped me to my feet again. I felt very weak, and was instantly attacked by vertigo. I leaned on her hard—so hard that it took all her strength to support me. We stood that way for a moment or two.

"The lamp," I said. "The rifle. . . ."

"I'll come back," she promised. "For everything."

She had something in her hand still, but she dropped it in order to help me stagger to the tent.

It was the flashgun.

Chapter 21

~~~~~~~~~~~~~~~~~

"The smell of blood," said Karen dourly, "might fetch every damn cat for miles."

"Unlikely," I said. "It jumped me because I was moving, not because I smell good. Human blood can't be a familiar prey-smell hereabouts."

"Neither was cooked meat," she pointed out.

"If you want to worry," I said, "worry. Just don't worry me."

We were back at the tent, outside. I was laid out on my sleeping bag. Karen had cleaned me up somewhat with the aid of river water boiled on the heater. The operation had not been pleasant for either of us. She didn't like handling something that looked like a piece of butchered meat. But she'd done it. Carefully and painstakingly. The cutting edge was back in her voice, now. But that was all right because I knew it wasn't aimed at me. It was fate that was pressing down on her. It was fate she was lashing out at.

The small lamp was still high in the branches, acting as a beacon. The big lamp, beside me, wasn't giving much light, but it was producing a lot of heat, keeping the cool of the night easily at bay. Karen was sitting in the mouth of the tent, cradling the rifle in her lap like a baby.

We'd both tried to sleep, on and off. We hadn't had much success. Tension was running too high. We were tired enough, but our minds weren't about to let go. And we were both afraid.

Of whatever might happen next.

I was feeling the pain as an unsteady force running over me. It was superficial. It seemed to move in time with the

151

wind in the treetops, cruel and uncertain, playing with my nerves and refusing me rest. When the wind blows, you have to grit your teeth and let it blow. There isn't anything you can do. I gritted my teeth, and let the pain flow, irresistible, unresisted.

"I could try to get the radio back," she said. "Raid the village."

"Single-handed?"

"I could try to get the medical kit, too."

"Or recruit a set of stretcher bearers."

"Maybe I could steal one of those boats."

"And paddle it upriver—through the rapids backwards?"

"So what the hell *do* we do?" she spat out, with some asperity.

"Wait," I said.

"For what?"

"A number ten bus."

One conversation, stone dead. It had never been a particularly healthy animal to start with. There wasn't much hope for any dialogue born of a situation like ours.

We waited.

Karen took me inside, soon after that, out of the reach of the flies. She maintained her own position, on watch in the doorway of the tent, for a little while more, but then came in and sealed the flap. The hours of the night continued on their resolute way outside, determined to take their own time no matter how we longed to be rid of them. She found the inner strength to surrender her talisman, the rifle, but she wouldn't ease her way into her sleeping bag. She remained on top of it. I don't know whether she slept—I suspect not—but she was still.

I looked back, in my mind, to the fright that had stranded me earlier, had left me marooned in time while the cat-thing stalked me. It seemed remote now, incomprehensible. All fear seemed alien to me now, even the fear which still lay awake in my mind: fear to death and disfigurement, of the uncertain day that was to follow. That fear was something that lay upon me, like a crumpled rag. It didn't seem to be part of the essential me.

My mind's eye was still in the forest. But it no longer saw a mass of grotesque and hostile shadows, replete with the ghosts that crept out from the failure of rational confrontation. It was something dead, now. Something distant. Something I could never get close to, no matter how I tried.

The whole meaning of the forest, as I perceived it, had changed. Its inner significance shifted, and could no longer be pinned down. The knowledge of the people of the forest and the metamorphosis which they had undergone had done that. They had taken the whole issue beyond understanding.

The hours dragged on, and I lost myself gradually in a liquid, placid delirium. One image perpetually returned to me—the image of the panther, suspended in mid-air, its little claws splayed, while simultaneously the lamp glowed distantly in the crown of the tree, caged in waxed wood, costumed in polished green leaves, a marker, a lure.

It was almost dawn when she came in through the flap. She moved silently, almost breathlessly. She might have been moving all night, going nowhere, seeing nothing, feeling her way, or she might have been close by for many hours, sleeping within the sound of the waves rippling against the river's shore.

It was dark in the tent. She couldn't see me. As she groped around I caught her wrist with the fingers of my left hand. They must have felt rough against her skin. She started.

"It's Alex," I whispered.

"I came back," she said, also whispering.

"I knew you would," I said.

"I didn't," she replied. "Not for a long time. That smell in the air—it did things to my mind. Before you shot me. Afterwards, I almost wished you hadn't. I think I might have torn off that mask. I don't know. It wasn't until then, afterwards, that I realized that it was the butterflies made them what they were. That fear, that repulsion, there was no need. If I could have . . ."

I waited my breathing very shallow. If Karen was listening, she was content to wait, content to hear what Mariel had to say.

"The butterflies," she added, "were so beautiful."

"I couldn't bear it," I said. "The magnification of my senses. I couldn't take it."

"I could," she said.

"Didn't it hurt?"

"Like fire, hell, but only in the beginning. After that it began to seem not so strange. I don't know why. I don't remember what I felt. When I woke up, it was lost. It didn't make any sense. But I knew, or maybe I didn't know anything. I was confused. I had to get away. I had to. The smell was still there, in the air. Just a ghost. It was strange in my head, and I couldn't quite grasp . . . something. I followed it. It didn't lead anywhere."

"It doesn't," I said. "Not to anywhere we want to go."

"You," she said.

"You too," I told her.

She wasn't sure.

"They . . ." she began, then faltered.

"It isn't the caterpillar that comes out of the cocoon," I said. "It's something that defies a caterpillar's understanding."

"If you *knew*," she said. "If *I* knew—it all seemed so very *possible*, just for a while."

"If I were a caterpillar," I said, "and I *knew*—if I had the choice. I wouldn't ever spin a chrysalis. I couldn't. It would be contrary to every caterpillar thing I knew."

"They chose," she said.

"No they didn't. They had no choice at all. Neither does the caterpillar. But you do. Those people, those aliens, may have the forest. But that's all they have and all they ever can have. In winning the forest, they lost all the things that made the forest attractive, the beautiful garden. When you're *in* the Garden of Eden, the myth makes no sense. It can't. It has to lose its meaning."

"I don't know," she said.

But she did. Inside herself.

"You came back," I said. "I knew you would. If only the drug hadn't blasted your mind, burned you out. You had to."

"Suppose," she said, "you hadn't got the mask on. Suppose you were too slow. We'd all be savages."

"Or dead. Or crawling back to the settlement with idiot stares in our faces. Maybe. But you're okay. You have more than the forest, still. Infinitely more. All the worlds of the stars. And you're only fourteen years old. You have a long life, Mariel."

"Fifteen," she said.

"What?"

"Fifteen. I've been fifteen for three weeks, on the ship's clock."

"You could have said."

"So you could send flowers? Or maybe hold a party, with jelly and ice cream?" She tried to capture the acid edge of Karen's voice, but she didn't make it. Her voice, by nature, was so much softer. She didn't sound nearly sarcastic enough. Only slightly forlorn.

She moved. Her free arm bumped my side and I winced. "What's the matter?" she said.

"I got hurt," I told her. "Cut up a bit. But now you're back, it should be okay. It may take a fortnight to get back, but we'll do it. With two shoulders to lean on. . . ." I broke off suddenly. "Why couldn't you tell?" I whispered. "Why didn't you know?"

"I can't see," she said. "I have to be able to see, or touch. Can I touch your face?"

I guided her hand to my forehead, away from the cuts.

"Well," I said. "Can you feel the wheels turning?"

"Your face," she said. Her hand hadn't move to touch the cuts on my cheek. "Your face is scarred."

"It doesn't matter," I said. "Compared with other things it really isn't that important."

Chapter 22

A great deal later—some months had passed—I stood at the crown of the hill in the tiny settlement, beside a crude cairn built of quarried stones. Nathan Parrick was with me.

"You'll not be leaving here with too many happy memories," he said.

"Will you?" I countered.

"Your arm . . ." he said, delicately.

I flexed the fingers to show him. "Maybe not as good as new," I said, "but it works. I may have to be back-handed for the rest of my life, but it's far from useless." I reached up to touch my cheek. "And as for these, sometimes I think they add character. I can get them fixed, back on Earth, tissue regrowth. But I might keep them. I don't know why, not for happy memories, that's for sure. But it's in faces that we perceive identities, and I'm not so sure that I should go home without a scar or two."

"That's a little bitter," he said.

"Must be the company I keep," I replied. "I used to be such a nice innocent fellow."

"What are you going to write in your report?" he asked, with sudden bluntness.

"What do *you* think?"

"I think you're still harboring some of that old conscientious resentment. I think you've kept it locked up in your heart since the day we landed, maybe even before that."

"This world should never have been colonized."

"I agree," he said.

"Good. Then our reports should be pretty much the same. Shouldn't they?"

"Maybe they should," he said. "But there might be two ways of going about it. It's not our job to apportion blame, you know."

"Like hell. It's up to us to analyze why this colony failed. I know why and so do you. Because the politicians played games. Dangerous games. They worked a trick, relieved pressure by sending out an under-equipped colony to a world rated as dangerous by the survey team, below the critical threshold of acceptable risk."

"And that's what you're going to say."

"That's what I'm going to say."

He leaned against the cairn. His eyes weren't on me, they were staring out over the vast expanse of the forest. "You've had a bad time here, Alex," he said.

"I bloody nearly died," I said. "If it hadn't been for Karen and Mariel. They got me back in one piece, slightly soiled but intact. And if we hadn't all been lucky, the political chicanery could have trapped us too, killed us just as it all but destroyed the colony. But that's not the whole issue, and you know it. There's no personal resentment in this."

"Yes there is," he contradicted me. "Not about your getting hurt, maybe. But there's a personal element which always clouds your objectivity. It always gets in your way.

I wish you could put it aside long enough to consider this as it lies."

I shrugged. "Okay," I said, sarcastically, "you tell me how it lies, how it looks from up there."

"What you want to do," he said, "is give Pietrasante and the UN the ammunition they need to get star travel started again on a meaningful scale. That's what I've been hired to do, as well. Let's take that for granted as our end, and think about means. Dendra looks bad, Alex. In many ways it's the worst possible advertisement we could have, far worse even than Kilner's colony. In the forest there are savages, without language and without fire. Not only that, but they're *white* savages, and even in this day and age that's a loaded point. The UN aren't going to like the idea of those savages, and neither are some of the governments they're going to have to ask for big contributions to funds. In the settlement, there are people hardly any better off. We've done a lot for them, as much as we can. We've mapped out some kind of way they can survive, begin to increase again. But we both know that it isn't any kind of permanent solution. They're safe up here, but up here is only one tiny enclave of a big world. Some time, they're going to go through it all again: the forest, the trap. There's precious little chance that they can thrive up here, expand, conquer the forest, even forewarned about the butterflies. Okay, we don't have to write down our misgivings. We say what we've done, we say that its *possible* that the colony can survive here indefinitely, maybe build towns and some kind of civilization, maybe one day recover sufficiently to make use of the stuff in the cylinder. But it still looks bad, Alex. It still looks bad."

"So what do we do? Tell lies?"

He shook his head. "No lies. We can't afford that. But we change the angle of attack. We look for a scapegoat. And it mustn't be the politicians. The one thing we mustn't do is put the blame where you want to put it."

"That's where it belongs."

"Maybe. In your eyes. I guess it does. But that's not the point. The point is that if you accuse the politicians you're accusing the very same organizations in some cases the very same committees—that we have to deal with when we get back. You blame the politicians, and you're blaming the UN itself. You're hitting out at the very thing that we're trying to rebuild: the means to achieve the resumption of starflight."

"The *political* means."

"The political means are the only ones that count. They're where the power lies. We have the technology, we even have the resources, what we lack is the organization, the collective will. And the one way to weaken that collective will is to attack the political structures necessary to it. If you try to make the UN and its filial organizations carry the can for what happened on this world, you'll be sabotaging our whole mission. Do you see that?"

I could feel a nasty taste in my mouth.

"So who do *you* want to blame?" I asked. "The colonists? Because they didn't have the collective will to stick together?"

"Oh no," he said, softly now. "Not the colonists. You still don't see, do you? There's only one place to lay the blame. We have to make the survey team the scapegoats. It's the only way."

"But the survey team was right!" I protested. "They *said* there were too many unknown factors. They advised against colonization. They were *right*."

"It doesn't count," he said. "Not now. They're the only pigeon we have. We have to say that they didn't do their job properly, that they could have and should have spotted the rogue factor. We have to say that it was all their fault, that their statements about unknown factors only add up to a cover-up, an excuse for a job that wasn't properly done."

"You bastard," I said.

"They're dead," he replied, calmly. "It can't hurt them. They're a hundred and fifty years dead."

"Scientists die," I answered, bitterly, "but politicians don't. Is that it?"

"Political institutions don't die," he said. "They're still alive. And we need them, desperately, on our side."

"And we have to whitewash them to get what we want?"

"That," he said, still in a tone that was deadly calm, "is the way it works. It's the only way."

"And that's what's going into your report?"

He turned from his contemplation of the forest, now, and his dark eyes bored into mine. "If we're to have any hope at all Alex, it has to be what goes into your report, too. At the very least, you mustn't write anything to contradict it."

I laughed, awkwardly. "What price honesty?" I said.

"I don't know, Alex," he said. "What price? Suppose the price is the failure of the mission, the abandonment of star travel for another fifty or five hundred years? Is that a price you're willing to pay? That's the decision you have to make. You and you alone."

"What about you?"

He shrugged. "I'm a professional. I do my job. I asked you to be a professional, too, Alex. Don't you remember?"

"I remember," I assured him. Now it was me that was staring out at the green ocean of treetops. I couldn't meet his gaze. It was all too much for me, a sickening double bind. I couldn't think of a way to hit back. No way at all.

I felt that it was all so unjust. But essentially, I accepted his argument. I could see what he meant.

And the stupid thing was that maybe, just maybe, Dendra wasn't a failure at all. In the UN sense, yes, but in a larger context the people of the forest had a chance. They could make a home here, make Dendra *their* world. It wasn't what the plan had intended, but it was *something*. To *me*, it was something.

But back on Earth, they not only wouldn't understand, they *couldn't*. To them, a naked savage was a total failure, something to be ashamed of. They didn't know what the word 'alien' meant. Their minds had never left the egocentric orbit from which they seemed to be the center of the universe and the focal point for judgment of all it contained. From where they sat, all of the star-worlds, if they were to be human worlds, had to be alternate Earths. Better Earths, maybe, but better in the narrow egocentric sense that was all they could imagine. Cleaner streets, better social services, more of the commercially packaged bliss they called happiness. Nothing essentially *different*.

"I think I know how Kilner felt," I said.

"Maybe," said Nathan. "And do you see where Kilner went wrong—why he failed Pietrasante and the people who sent him out?"

"We have to *make them see*," I said. "We have to make them *understand*."

"There's no way we'll even get the opportunity," he said. "We have to do it their way. It's their game, their rules."

"They're the wrong rules."

"Maybe," he said, again. His equanimity was still not shaken.

He turned round to look at the pile of stones he'd been leaning on. "Do you think this was right?" he asked. I could tell from the tone of his voice that the other subject was closed. He was on a different wavelength now. "Do you think it was right to bury it again?"

"We had no real right to dig it up," I said. "It wasn't addressed to us. They can't use it. Nor their children, nor their children's children. Maybe one day, in a hundred or a thousand years, they'll have the basics again—the basics to build on. They'll be able to use it then."

"And if they can't," said Nathan. "Perhaps . . ."

He didn't finish. I shook my head. We both knew what I meant. The people of the forest wouldn't be back. They wouldn't dig it up. It wouldn't be any conceivable use to them if they did. Not until they'd gone through their own long cycle of evolution, become genuinely part of the forest, and populated the face of the planet with their own kind, their own alien kind. That wouldn't be a matter of hundreds of years. More likely of millions. And even steel rots.

But who could tell? We could only do whatever we did for the here and now, and leave eternity to the dictates of chance and destiny.

I looked back at the settlement. There were people moving between the buildings. No one was staring at us, we had long since come to be taken for granted. They were healthy people now, still simple-minded, but equipped so far as we could equip them with the means to keep themselves alive. They still remained a pitiful sight, and would always seem, to me at least, a doomed people, with no real future on Dendra. But we couldn't take them with us. We had to leave them suspended between the jaws of their trap.

Not all problems have solutions. Even when you know all the answers.

"Come on," said Nathan, "we'll be light-years from here by this time tomorrow. It'll all be behind us. Forever."

With the fingers of my right hand I traced the line of the four parallel scars which ran down the right side of my face, from beneath the lower eyelid almost to the edge of the jaw.

"Maybe," I said.

I didn't mean it.